KU-658-084

BROWN ON RESOLUTION

By the Same Author

PAYMENT DEFERRED
DEATH TO THE FRENCH
TWO AND TWENTY
PLAIN MURDER
THE GUN

THE BODLEY HEAD

BROWN ON RESOLUTION

BY

C. S. FORESTER

LONDON
JOHN LANE THE BODLEY HEAD

THIS EDITION FIRST PUBLISHED IN 1935

MADE AND PRINTED IN GREAT BRITAIN BY TONBRIDGE PRINTERS LTD.
PEACH HALL WORKS TONBRIDGE KENT

BROWN ON RESOLUTION

BROWN ON RESOLUTION

CHAPTER I

LEADING SEAMAN ALBERT BROWN lay dying on Resolution. He was huddled in a cleft in the grey-brown lava of which that desolate island is largely composed, on his back with his knees half-drawn up in his fevered delirium. Sometimes he would mumble a few meaningless words and writhe feebly on to his side, only to fall back again a second later. He was dressed in what had once been a sailor's suit of tropical white, but now it was so soiled and stained and draggled, so torn and frayed, as literally to be quite unrecognizable—it was now only a few thin, filthy rags feebly held together. His face was swollen and distorted, as were his hands, being quite covered with hideous lumps as a result of the poisoned bites of a myriad flies—a little cloud of which hung murderously over him as he lay, combining with the shimmering reek of the sun-scorched rock almost to hide him from view.

His feet, too, although a few fragments of what were once shoes still clung to them, were horribly swollen and bruised and cut. They were more like sodden lumps of raw horse-flesh than human feet. Not the cruellest human being on earth could have contemplated those dreadful feet without a throb of pity.

Yet a very cursory inspection of Albert Brown's dying body would be enough to show that he was not dying because of the biting flies, nor even because of the hideous condition of his feet. For the dingy rags on his right shoulder were stained a sinister brown, and when he turned on his side he revealed the fact that those at his back were similarly stained, and a closer look through the tatters of cloth would discover that Brown's right breast was covered with a black, oozing clot of blood like an empty football bladder hanging from a bullet wound over Brown's third rib.

Brown lay at the edge of the central, lifeless portion of the island. Mounting up above him rose the bare lava of the highest point of Resolution, a distorted muddle of naked rock bearing a million million razor edges—razor edges which readily explained the frightful condition of his feet. Just at Brown's level, stretching along at each side (for Resolution is a hog-backed island bent into a half-moon) began the cactus, ugly, nightmarish plants, like bottle-nosed pokers, clustering together thicker and thicker on the lower slopes, each bearing a formidable armament of spikes which explained the tattered condition of Brown's clothes. Frequently, stretched out in the scanty line of shade cast by the cacti, there lay iguanas—mottled crested lizards—somnolently stupid. Overhead wheeled sea-birds, and occasionally a friendly mocking-bird, strayed up from the lower slopes, would hop close round Brown's dying body and peer at him in seeming sympathy. Down at the water's edge, where the Pacific broke against the lava boulders, there massed a herd of marine iguanas—fantastic creatures which bear only their Latin generic name—industriously gnawing the seaweed on which they live, while round them strayed marvellous scarlet crabs and the other representatives of the amphibious life of this last, almost unknown member of the Galapagos Islands.

The sky above was of a glaring, metallic blue, in which hung a burnished sun that seemed to be pouring a torrent of molten heat upon the tortured fragment of land beneath it. The sea was of a kindlier blue, and far out near the horizon could be seen a grey line stretching out of sight in both directions, which marked the edge of an ocean current, haunted by sea-birds in hundreds, gathered there to revel in the food, living and dead, which clustered along this strange border.

No trace of human life could be seen around the whole wide horizon, save only for Leading Seaman Albert Brown, huddled in his cleft, and hunger and thirst and fever and loss of blood were soon to make an end even of him, the sole representative of the human race in all this wide expanse; perhaps in years to come some exploring scientist would happen across his bleached bones and would ponder over that broken rib and that smashed shoulder-blade. It is doubtful, though, whether he would explain them.

CHAPTER II

IT all began more than twenty years earlier, with Lieut.-Commander R. E. S. Saville-Samarez, R.N., seated in the train which was carrying him from the Royal Naval College, Greenwich, and a not very arduous course of professional study therein, towards London and a not very closely planned week of relaxation therein. He sat in his first-class carriage and looked, now at his newspaper, now out of the window, now up at the carriage roof, now at the lady who was seated demurely in the diametrically opposite corner of the carriage. For the Commander was not much given to prolonged reading, nor to prolonged following of any one train of thought. He thought, as was only natural, of the influence of first-class certificates upon promotion, and from that he passed to the consideration of Seniority versus Selection, and the Zone System, and he wondered vaguely if he would ever attain the comfortable security and majestic authority of Captain's rank with its consequent inevitable climb upwards to the awesome heights of an Admiral's position. Admirals in one way were mere commonplaces to the Commander, for he came of a long line of naval ancestors, and an uncle of his was an Admiral at that moment, and his grandfather had commanded a ship of the line at Cronstadt during the Crimean War, and *his* grandfather had fought at the Nile and had been an Admiral during the reign of George IV.

But he did not think long about Admirals, for he felt oddly restless and fidgety, and he wished that the lady was not in his carriage so that he could put his feet up on the opposite seat and smoke. He glanced across at her, and found, to his surprise, that she was contemplating him in a manner difficult to describe —detached yet friendly; certainly not in the way a lady ought to look at a man (even if it is granted she might look at all) with whom she was alone in a railway carriage in the year of our Lord 1893. The Commander was quite startled; he looked away, but his eyes strayed back, stealthily and shyly, as soon as he was sure her gaze was averted. No, she was not at all *that* sort—no one could be with that placid, calm look, almost like a nun's. But she was a fine woman, for all that, with her stylish sailor hat on the top of her head with a feather at the back, and her smart costume with its leg-of-mutton sleeves and her white collar, and the toe of one neat shoe just showing beneath her skirt as she sat. A fine upstanding figure of a woman, in fact, trim-waisted and corseted with correct severity. As he looked, she turned and met his gaze again, and he flushed with shy embarrassment down his sunburnt neck and hurriedly looked out of the window. But once again his eyes stole back again, inevitably. And she was smiling at him.

Agatha Brown's father was a Nonconformist greengrocer; but, as his Nonconformist friends would hurriedly explain when speaking of him, a greengrocer in a very large line of business. His big shop at Lewisham employed a dozen assistants, and he had two other shops besides, at Woolwich and Deptford, and the wealthy residents of the big houses of Blackheath always came to him for such delicacies as asparagus and early strawberries. He even handled a little wholesale trade, and long ago he had climbed high enough to leave off living over his shop and to take instead a substantial house beside Greenwich Park and furnish it in the best manner of the 1880's. Here he lived with his three sons and his daughter (his eldest child) who managed the house in the efficient and spacious manner possible in that era. His wife was dead and much regretted, but, thanks to Agatha's domestic efficiency, not much missed in the economic sphere.

That morning at breakfast Agatha had not felt any premonition of what was going to be the most marvellous day of her life. She had risen at her usual hour of 6.30, and had helped one maid with the breakfast while the other looked to the fires. She had poured out tea for Will and Harry and sat at table with them while they hurried through breakfast, and had closed her eyes and clasped her hands devoutly when Dad, having come back with George in the trap from market, read prayers what time the other two stood impatiently waiting to get off to their business of managing the Woolwich and Deptford shops. Then Dad, too, ate his breakfast, and it was then that Agatha had the first inkling that it was time something happened to her. Dad of course read his newspaper, and of course being preoccupied with that he could not attend properly to his table manners. With the newspaper propped up against the marmalade jar he would bring his mouth down to his fork rather than his fork up to his mouth, and he would open the latter alarmingly (which was quite unpleasant when, as was usual, he had not quite swallowed the preceding mouthful) and thrust the fork home and snap down his big moustache upon it in the way he always did, which Agatha found on this particular morning to be positively distressing. He drank his tea, too, noisily, through his moustache, and although Agatha had listened to the performance daily for twenty-nine years somehow she found it unusually distasteful. She found herself telling herself that it was time she had a change, and realizing on the instant that although she was that very day going for five days' stay with a bosom friend at Ealing that amount of change would not suffice her. Her first reaction was to promise herself a dose of senna that evening (senna was Agatha's prescription for all the ills flesh is heir to) and her second, amazingly, was to consider senna inadequate. Only slightly introspective though she was, Agatha found herself surprised at being in such an odd frame of mind.

Then when Dad had taken his departure Agatha had busied herself with the stupendous task of leaving everything in the house prepared for her five days' absence. She went round and paid the tradesmen's books. She instructed the cook very positively as to all the menus to come; she enjoined upon the housemaid the necessity to turn out the drawing-room on Tuesday and the dining-room on Wednesday, and Mr. Brown's bedroom and Mr. George's bedroom on Thursday and Mr. Harry's bedroom and Mr. Will's bedroom on Friday. She did her share of the morning's work; she lunched, as was her habit, excessively lightly, and when the afternoon came round she made herself ready for departure. At four o'clock she left the house with her little suit-case. She felt light-hearted and care-free; the tingle of her clean starched underlinen was pleasant to her; she was free of the house and all its troubles for five whole days; but all the same she did not want to spend five days at the home of Adeline Burton at Ealing. The old great friendship between Agatha and Adeline had of course cooled a little with the coming of maturity and with the migration of the Burton family to Ealing, and the Burton household was very like the Brown household, when all was said and done. But, still, Agatha felt strangely light-hearted as she walked to the station; she hummed a little song; and then she found herself in the same carriage as Lieut.-Commander R. E. S. Saville-Samarez.

She liked him, at first sight, and at first sight she knew him for what he was, a naval officer of the best brand of British stupidity. She liked his good clothes and his smooth cheeks (Agatha, as she regarded these last, felt a revulsion of feeling against the fashionable hairiness of 1893) and the way he blushed when she caught him looking at her. She knew he would speak to her soon, and she knew she would answer him.

Agatha's smile set the coping-stone on Samarez's unsettledness. He positively jumped in his seat. Automatically his hands fluttered to his pockets.

"Mind if I smoke?" he asked hoarsely.

"Not at all," said Agatha. "I should like it."

That, of course, was at least four words more than any lady ought to have said. Samarez feverishly pulled out his silver cigarette-case and match-box, lit a cigarette with fingers which were nearly trembling, and drew a lungful of smoke deep into himself in an unthinking effort after self-control.

Agatha was still smiling at him, the placid, innocent smile one would expect to see on the face of a nun or a mother. Samarez simply had to go on talking to her, and the Englishman's invariable opening topic came to his lips like an inspiration.

"Beastly weather," he said, with a nod through the carriage window, where February sunshine fought a losing battle against February gloom.

" I rather like it, somehow," said Agatha. She would have liked any weather at the moment. " Of course you find it very different from the tropics," she went on, to Samarez's amazement. How on earth could she tell he had been to the tropics ?

" Er—yes," he said. " Beastly hot there, sometimes."

" China Station ? " she asked. Agatha's knowledge of the Navy was only what might be expected of a secluded young woman of the middle class of 1893, but she had heard the blessed words " China Station " somewhere and they drifted into her mind now and were seized upon gratefully.

" Yes," said Samarez, more amazed than ever, " that was last commission."

The China Station was a pleasant source of conversation. Thanks to the exaltation of her mood, Agatha was able to talk—or rather to induce Samarez to talk—without displaying any annoying ignorance, and by the blessing of Providence they chatted really amicably for a few minutes. Samarez's heart warmed to this charming woman, so refined, so friendly without being cheap, with such a musical contralto voice and such a ready laugh. Stations came and stations went unheeded, and Samarez was quite surprised when he peered out of the window and saw that they had reached London Bridge—London Bridge on a dark, damp, February evening. With a little chill of disappointment he realized that in a few minutes he would have to separate from this friend. He deemed himself fortunate even that she was travelling on to Charing Cross.

Friends at the moment were scarce. Samarez had a week's leave on his hands, and he was almost at a loss as to how to employ it. He had had in mind dinner at the Junior Rag, possibly an encounter with an acquaintance, and a seat at a musical comedy afterwards. But he had done that for several evenings already, previous to his course at Greenwich, and the prospect bored him, nearly unborable as he was. On the China Station, stifling under the awnings, the most delectable spot on earth had appeared to be the dining-room of the Junior Army and Navy Club, but now it did not seem half so attractive.

And, above all, Agatha Brown was a woman, well fleshed and desirable to the eye of 1893. Women did not count for much in Samarez's life; marriage, of course, was unthinkable to a man of his sturdy devotion to his profession, and his contact with other women had been slight and nearly forgotten. But—but the urge was there, unadmitted but overwhelming. Samarez at present had nothing more in his mind than companionship. He wanted to talk to a woman—to this woman, now that he had made the first impossible plunge. He wanted neither men's talk nor solitude. He would have been scared by his intensity of emotion had he had a moment in which to realize it—but he had not. They had rattled through Waterloo Junction, and were rumbling on to Charing Cross railway bridge. Through the window he could see the wide, grey river, and the lights of Charing Cross Station were close at hand. Agatha glanced up at her suit-case on the rack, in evident mental preparation for departure. Samarez stood up in the swaying carriage; his hands flapped with embarrassment.

"L—look here," he said, "we don't want

to say good-bye yet. Oh, we don't. Let's—let's come and have dinner somewhere."

He stood holding to the luggage rack, appalled by his realization that he had definitely committed himself, that he was guilty (if the lady chose to find him so) of an ungentlemanly action. His innocent eyes pleaded for him. And Agatha's eyes softened ; he was so like an artless little boy begging for more cake. She felt motherly and not a bit daring as she said yes.

Once out of the train Samarez, despite his stupefied elation, displayed all the orderly logic of deed of the disciplined man of action. Agatha's suit-case and his own leather kit-bag were ticketed-in at the cloak-room, a cab was summoned, and with a flash of brilliance he recalled the name of the one restaurant which in those bleak days was suitable for ladies and at the same time was tolerant of morning dress. The cab-horse's hoofs clattered across the station courtyard and out into the Strand, and they sat side by side as the lamps went by.

Pleasant it was, and each was conscious of a comforting warmth from the other. Each felt supremely befriended and most deliciously expectant—of what, they could not say. The drive passed all too quickly; to Agatha it hardly seemed a moment before she found herself being helped from the cab by the whiskered and uniformed restaurant porter.

From opposite sides of the table each regarded the other, seemingly with some slight misgiving regarding their good fortune. It was too good to be true, for the one that he should be sitting with and talking dazzlingly to a woman of good sense and irreproachable morals (to a sailor such an encounter is all too rare an occurrence), and for the other that she should be in a restaurant at all (this was nearly Agatha's first experience of restaurants) let alone with a clean-bred, good-looking young man opposite her. Samarez ordered a good dinner—trust him for that—and summoned the wine waiter. The very mention of the word "wine" caused Agatha to start a little in her chair, for the worthy Mr. Brown was a staunch, true-blue, even violent, abstainer, who would not allow villainous alcohol even the shelter of his roof. But here of course, amid the gilding and the gay people and the supple-backed waiters, it was all different.

"Choose for yourself," said Agatha, as Samarez looked across at her from the wine list.

Dinner passed by in a delicious dream. Agatha's acquaintance with food so far had been of the roast-beef and apple-tart order. When she consulted Mrs. Beeton, it had been for the purpose of designing substantial and unambitious meals for the hearty Browns, who one and all, following in Mr. Brown's footsteps, lost no opportunity of expressing their contempt for what they termed "made dishes." So far the subtleties of sauces and the refinements of foods had passed Agatha by, so that now each succeeding course lingering brilliantly upon the palate came as a new and delicious revelation. Not even the necessity of tactfully observing which implements Samarez employed and imitating his example could mar her enjoyment, and the wine, with its unaccustomed influence, warming and comforting and heartening, was the finishing touch. She leant forward towards Samarez and talked without a care, and he talked back with what seemed to him to be positively dazzling wit. They made a good pair; Agatha with her smooth cheeks and bright eyes and upright figure, Samarez bronzed and blond and clean-looking, with the far-seeing expression in his grey eyes which characterizes the majority of sailors. He was very young for his years; even though, as Agatha realized with a pang of regret, he was actually younger than she was. And once or twice his head went back and he chuckled deep down in his chest with wrinkles round his eyes in a manner which brought a great big pain into Agatha's breast, and made her long to stretch out her barren arms and draw his rough head down to her bosom. She found herself imagining herself rubbing her cheek against his short rebellious hair, and the mere thought turned her faint with longing as she sat in her chair, strangely maternal.

"Well, I'm blest," said the Commander suddenly. "Do you know, I've been talking to you all this time and I don't even know what your name is?"

"It's Agatha," said Agatha—that much of

her name was tolerable to her, although the " Brown " always rankled—" and I don't know yours either."

Samarez hesitated for one regretted second; he was sure that it was unwise to tell one's name to a strange woman, but this woman was so different.

" It's a very long one," he said, " but it begins with Richard."

" Of course it would," said Agatha bewilderingly, " and they call you Dickie, don't they ? "

" They used to," admitted Samarez, " but they mostly call me Sammy nowadays, men do."

" Then I shall call you Dickie," said Agatha decidedly, and she finished her coffee as though to seal the bargain.

So dinner was finished, and the room was beginning to throng with more sensible people dining at a more reasonable hour. They had no possible excuse for lingering on, and yet they both of them were most desperately unwilling to part. Their eyes met again and again across the table, and conversation died a fevered death, and neither could voice what each had most in mind. Agatha simply did not know the usual gambits leading up to the making of a new appointment; Samarez with an odd touch of sensitiveness felt that it would be banal and discordant to speak about it—this was not an ordinary woman. The restaurant was growing crowded; the waiter brought his bill unasked, and hovered round the table with the unmistakable intention of showing them that the management would prefer to see them make way for fresh comers. Fate simply forced them, with sinking hearts, to rise from the table with the words unspoken. Samarez waited for her in the foyer in a really restless and unsettled state of mind.

And Agatha, adjusting her veil in the cloak-room, felt on the verge of tears. She had been most wildly unladylike; she had talked with strange men in gilded halls of vice; it was past seven o'clock and she really must reach Ealing and the Burtons' by nine at the latest; and she did not want to leave Dickie. Most emphatically she did not want to. But she had not the faintest idea of what she did want.

At the door circumstances forced them further towards separation.

" Cab, I suppose ? " said Samarez huskily.

They climbed into a four-wheeler, and Samarez, still retaining a grain of sanity, directed the driver to Charing Cross Station. Agatha had clean forgotten the luggage left there. The cab wormed its way through the clattering traffic and turned into Chandos Street, dim-lighted and quiet. Restlessly Samarez took off his hat and wiped his fretted forehead. A passing street lamp showed up his boyish face and his rumpled hair.

" Oh," said Agatha uncontrollably. One hand went to his shoulder, the other fumbled for his lean brown hand in the darkness. Samarez turned clumsily with his arms out to her, and all their unhappiness melted away under their wild kisses.

CHAPTER III

IT was the lights of the Strand and of the courtyard entrance at Charing Cross which brought them back momentarily to reality. Agatha's face was wet with tears, her hat hung by one hatpin, as their embrace came to an end. The cab halted outside the station and a porter tore open the door.

"I—I can't get out," stammered Agatha, shrinking away into a corner.

Samarez climbed out and shut the door.

"Wait!" he flung at the driver, and pelted into the station, dragging out the luggage receipt from his pocket as he hastened to the cloak-room with fantastic strides, blinded by the lights. By the grace of Providence there was no one there awaiting attention; it was only a matter of seconds before he came back, suit-case and kit-bag in hand. He opened the door of the cab, and Agatha came to life again out of her mazed dream.

"Where to, sir?" asked the cab-driver.

"Where to?" echoed Samarez stupidly.

"I don't know—Ealing, I suppose," said a little voice from the depths of the cab.

"Ealing," said Samarez to the cab-driver.

"Ealing, sir? Ealing Broadway, sir? Right, sir," said the cab-driver, and round came the horse and the door slammed to, with Samarez and Agatha in blessed solitude once more, happily ignorant of the meaning wink of the cab-driver and the broad grins of the porters It was quite several seconds before hand met hand and lip met lip again in the velvet darkness of the cab, while the horse's hoofs clip-clopped solidly onwards towards Ealing.

Passion had them greatly in thrall. Agatha's hat was off by now, and the tears flowed freely from her eyes as she pressed against Samarez with all the abandon her corseted waist permitted. Agatha had forgotten she was twenty-nine, of strict Wesleyan upbringing. Twenty-nine years of bottled-up emotion were tearing her to pieces; some faint, unknown cause had obscurely begun the explosion—perhaps even before she had met Samarez—and there was no power on earth that could check it now before it had run its course. She gave herself up to him in an ecstasy of giving.

As for Samarez there is less to be said. He at least had known kisses before, and the encirclement of a woman's arms was not quite new to him. Even purchased caresses ought to have given him sufficient experience to have told him whither they were straying, but reaction from loneliness and the fierce insistent urge of his sex had swept him away. Agatha's sweet flesh in his arms and the touch of her unpractised lips on his mouth were all the facts of which he was conscious at the moment. He never dreamed of discretion while he let his instincts carry him away in the darkness, and he pressed her hotly.

Somehow or other Agatha found herself speaking, her hands on his breast and her face lifted to his.

"Of course, I've *got* to go to Ealing," she said. It was a statement doomed to extinction at birth, made automatically in an automatic hope of contradiction.

"What are you going to do there?" asked Samarez.

"I'm going to stay with friends. They're expecting me."

The little voice whispering in the darkness added fresh fuel to the flames of Samarez's passion. Into the back of his mind leapt the sudden realization that in the cab with them, beside them on the other seat, lay her luggage and his, all their necessaries for days.

"Can't you put them off?" he asked, hardly realizing what he was saying. "Send them a wire. Don't go."

"Oh, my *dear*," came the answering whisper.

Let it not be imagined that Agatha acted in ignorance. At twenty-nine, when one is an old maid and busy with Chapel work, one hears things. Married women say things just as if one were married oneself, and Chapel work sometimes brings one into contact with illegitimate motherhood and even sometimes undisguised adultery. Agatha knew quite well what happened when a man "stayed with" a woman—at least, she had a general idea of it even if she were hazy as to detail. So that her wordless consent to Samarez's fierce suggestion, and her acquiescence when Samarez leaned out of the window and redirected the cabman, were absolutely inexcusable, so her fellow-workers would think. But her fellow-workers had never known, perhaps would never know, the careless, happy stupefaction of sudden passion.

The hotel porter was discreet; the hotel reception clerk was friendly; in fact, no one in the hotel thought twice about them, because Agatha looked the last person in the world to share a bedroom with a man who was not her husband, and her glove concealed the absence of a wedding-ring. In the dignified seclusion of the hotel bedroom Samarez's enforced calm fell away from him like a discarded garment. He opened his arms to her and she came gladly to them, giving herself with a delicious, cool relaxation. She still felt fantastically motherly towards this tousle-headed boy even during his greediest caresses, and when he sighed out his content with his face upon her bosom she clasped him against it with the same gesture as she would have used to a child.

And the next day, and the day after, and the day after that this maternal attitude became more and more marked. She was so many years older than he, she felt. The sheer physical longing she had felt for him had given way to a stranger, calmer affection. She seemed to have grown suddenly used to him. It was odd, but true. No twinge of conscience came to ruffle the serenity of her soul; she was flooded with a sense of well-being that was not diminished by the necessity for practical arrangements, such as writing to Adeline Burton a careful letter explaining that an unforeseen domestic crisis had compelled her reluctantly to postpone her visit at such brief notice as to prevent her even from letting her know. Agatha would come some other time, as soon as she could, if Adeline did not mind. The lies which Agatha wrote flowed so naturally from her pen that she did not give them a thought—to Agatha's mind the aged aunt suddenly stricken with mortal illness and demanding immediate nursing seemed to be an actual living character. She did not even feel relieved that Greenwich and Ealing should be so far apart as to render it quite impossible for Adeline to discover by a casual call that no such lady existed.

Samarez, on the other hand, was very puzzled

and almost uncomfortable of conscience on those occasions when it occurred to him to think what he was doing, and to make deductions from the somewhat meagre data presented to him. Agatha had never "been there before"; he was sure of that for more reasons than one. No one could have been, anyway, and still retained the blossoming innocence which she displayed at every moment. She clearly had not even toyed with the idea of dallying with men. Her underclothing proved that, if nothing else did. It was exquisitely neat, with a myriad tucks and gatherings, but it was not to be called frivolous. It was even pathetic in its lack of sex appeal. Just the sort of white, longcloth underclothing a nun would wear, if (Samarez had no information on the point) nuns wore underclothing. Samarez's knowledge of underclothing was limited; but in those days it was only daughters of joy who wore garments other than virgin white and strove after ornament as well as utility. And Agatha's pathetically severe nightgown, high-buttoned and severe and undecorated, settled that matter to Samarez's mind. So that Agatha was a respectable member of a respectable family, who had bestowed her virginity on him just as she might have given half a crown to a beggar. It made Samarez queerly uncomfortable. And yet, after three days' intimacy, she was far less attainable than ever before. Samarez could feel no thrill of pride of possession while he was with her, not even in the most triumphant moments of intimacy. Something was still out of reach, beyond attainment, and he was piqued in consequence. He tried to buy presents for her, to lavish money on her for clothes and jewellery, but whenever he tried she put the suggestion aside with a smiling, irresistible negative. Poor Samarez was not to know that Agatha's main reason for refusal was the impossibility of subsequently explaining away these gifts to her family.

So it was with a queer mixture of pique and gentlemanly feeling that, after three days, Samarez proposed marriage to her. He did not want to; he held the strongest possible opinion regarding the unsuitability of marriage for naval officers, and he did not believe in marriage much, anyway. But he proposed, and as he did so he regarded her anxiously with expectant eyes, at the same moment annoyed with himself for throwing away his future and comforted by the knowledge that he was doing the "right thing." And Agatha, her hands on his shoulders, looked deep into those anxious eyes before she slowly shook her head.

"No, Dickie," she said, "it would be better if we didn't. But it was awfully nice of you to ask me."

Then she strained him impulsively to her, and kissed him hotly. She saw the unwisdom of marrying a man whom one only loved as one might love a pet St. Bernard, and who would never be able to claim that entire devotion and subservience which Agatha, in accordance with the ideas of the time, thought she ought to give to her husband. But she was keenly alive to the extent of the sacrifice Samarez had proposed making, and appreciative of it.

So that after five days the affair came to an end. Five days during which Agatha had had a glimpse of the sort of life led by women who are not greengrocers' daughters; five days of theatres (an annual pantomime and an annual circus was the nearest Agatha had ever come to a theatre until then), of good food, of leisure, of ample spendings. Truth to tell, the waste of money and time, by the end of the five days, had so worked upon Agatha's mind that she was quite glad of the prospect of returning home to economical housekeeping and domestic industry. And Samarez had begun to cease to interest her—he was not a tremendously interesting fellow, as a matter of fact.

Yet the parting was painful. Samarez did not want her to go; he clung to her as they kissed good-bye in the hotel bedroom, with his hand to her breast. He felt almost humble and subdued, almost frightened at the prospect of two days' loneliness before rejoining his ship; and Agatha's eyes were wet, too, although she realized she was doing the sensible thing, and it was very gently that she put his hands aside and turned away. He held her hand in the cab as they drove to Charing Cross, and he even tried to make one last appeal after she had boarded the train for Greenwich. She only shook her head and smiled, however, and two minutes later Samarez was alone on the platform, watching the train round the bend in the distance, trying obstinately not to feel relieved.

It was the end of the incident for him. In later years he forgot what his own attitude had been, and he only remembered it as a rather pleasant and unusual encounter, which he would like to repeat with some one else (he never did). Sometimes, years later, in expansive moments, he would tell other men of his strange meeting with "quite a nice, well-brought-up woman, a lady, you know," with whom he had stayed five delightful days at Benjamin's Hotel, who had refused all his presents except the wedding-ring they had found it advisable to buy, and whose surname and address he had never known. The other men would be incredulous and envious, and Samarez, Commander Samarez or Captian Samarez or Admiral Samarez, as he came to be, would pull down his waistcoat and plume himself upon his unusual good fortune and dexterity.

CHAPTER IV

AGATHA arrived home to find everything quite normal, save for the inevitable deterioration of efficiency consequent upon the mistress's absence. No hint had reached the Browns that she had not been staying with the Burtons, and she told one or two placid lies regarding these latter, which gave a little local colour to the idea that she had been there; and, as lying was unusual to her, she almost came to believe she had been there. For her exalted mood died away. Within a week it seemed incredible to her that she could have been guilty of such terrible conduct; she had forgotten the state of mind which had led her into it; she felt and hoped that it had only been a very vivid and shocking dream. She ceased in consequence to carry the ring Samarez had bought her on the ribbon round her neck.

Yet very soon she became actively aware that it was not a dream, could not have been a dream. For a time she thrust her fears behind her and went on grimly with her household affairs, but they continually recurred to her. She was worried about them, and uncertain of what she ought to do. She knew Samarez's name and ship (of course she would!) and for a moment thought of writing to him, but she put the idea aside as unworthy. But as the symptoms became unmistakable and she began to fear discovery she grew more worried, and it was a positive relief when the storm broke. Mr. Brown came home one day at five—rather earlier than his usual time.

"No, I don't want any tea," he said, and there was that in his voice which told Agatha what he knew.

"Come here, my girl," went on Mr. Brown. "I want to talk to you."

"Well?" said Agatha, quite calm and steady now that the crisis had come.

"I met Burton this afternoon, quite by accident. And he said—he said he was sorry to hear about my sister, and what a pity it was that you weren't able to go over to Ealing and stay there the last time it was arranged."

Mr. Brown stared at his daughter from under his heavy eyebrows. The thing was incredible to him—and yet—and yet—his doubts led him to work himself up into a rage.

"Didn't you tell me last February you were going to stay there, and didn't you come back and say you had?" he blared.

"Yes," said Agatha.

"Well, where did you get to? Where the *devil* did you get to?"

Agatha made no reply.

"You made me look such a bleeding fool when Burton said that to me," raved Mr. Brown—the adjective showed he was nearly beside himself. "Where the devil did you get to?"

The horrible and incredible doubts which had assailed him and which he had put aside as quite impossible renewed themselves and goaded him into frightful agitation.

"Was—was it a *man?*" he demanded. "Tell me this minute, girl."

Agatha knew that it was no use telling Mr.

Brown about Samarez. He wouldn't understand. She didn't understand herself.

"My God, it was!" said Mr. Brown. "Who was it? What filthy swine——?"

He mouthed and spluttered with rage.

"Who was it? Was it young Evans?"

Evans was the local roué, a greasy-haired young man whom Agatha hated. The suggestion was so comic that Agatha had to smile, and the smile increased her father's frenzy.

"Who was it? Tell me, or I'll——"

"It wasn't anybody you know, dad," said Agatha.

"Damned if I care. Tell me his name and I'll find him. I'll teach him."

"No you won't, dad, I won't tell you."

"You won't? We'll see, my girl."

"Yes, we'll see," said Agatha. Her old exalted mood was coming over her again, leaving her outwardly calm and placid and nunlike, but inwardly rejoicing. Mr. Brown stared at her serene face, and his rage simmered down into incredulous astonishment.

"Who the devil was it, if it wasn't Evans?" he pleaded pitifully.

"It was some one else," said Agatha quite calmly, looking over his head at something a thousand miles distant.

"But—but he didn't do you any *harm*, Aggie, old girl, did he?" wheedled Mr. Brown.

Agatha met his eyes, and nodded with certitude.

"You would say he did, dad," said Agatha.

The flush of Mr. Brown's anger gave way to a yellow pallor. His very bulk as he sat in his sacred chair seemed to diminish.

"You don't mean that, do you, dear?" he asked quite unnecessarily, for he knew she did.

Later he gave way to pathetic helplessness.

"What am I to do?" he pleaded. "What ever will the Chapel say?"

Upon Mr. Brown dawned the awful realization that despite his three shops, despite his wholesale connection, despite his fine house and solid furniture, the Chapel would find huge stores of food for gossip in this terrible catastrophe. The finger of scorn would be pointed at him; he would never be able to hold up his head again. Never more would the proud privilege be his of passing round the plate at morning service.

The arrival of his two eldest sons prolonged the discussion. Will and Harry were brimful of the ferocious energy which had carried their father to such heights in the world of greengrocery, and, unlike him, they were still young and able to reach instant, Napoleonic decisions.

"People mustn't know about it," said Will positively, "that's certain. Agatha will have to go away for the—as soon as it's necessary. We'll have to say she's gone to stay with friends in Edinburgh or somewhere."

"That's it," chimed in Harry, "and the—the child will have to be boarded out when she comes back. It ought to be easy enough."

The three of them looked to Agatha for agreement, and found none. Her face was as though cut in stone. The bare thought of having her child "boarded out," the child for whom she was ready, even anxious, to endure so much, was like a savage blow in the face.

"No," she said, "I won't have him boarded out. I'm going to be with him, always."

The pronoun she used displayed her silly,

baseless hope that her child would be a son, but it passed unnoticed and uncommented upon.

"Don't be silly," said Harry, with immense scorn. "Of course we must board the child out—if it lives."

The thought and the wish that fathered it tore at Agatha's heart-strings.

"Oh, how I hate you!" she burst out. "Of course he's going to live. And I am going to keep him too. Don't you dare say anything else!"

"Pooh!" sneered Will. "You'll have to do what you're told. Beggars can't be——"

Will's speech broke off short as he caught sight of the flash of triumph in Agatha's face, and was reminded by it of a forgotten factor in the argument. He met the eyes of his father and his brother with some uneasiness.

For fifteen years ago, when Mr. Brown had just begun to be successful in business, he had followed the prudent example of thousands of others by investing his savings in house property and deeding it over to his wife. That, of course, had been in the days before limited liability, and was a wise precaution ensuring the possession of capital and the necessaries of life even if bankruptcy were to strip Mr. Brown nominally of all he possessed. Mr. Brown had seen to it that his wife made a will in his favour, and had thought no more about it. Until at his wife's death; for then, as soon as Mrs. Brown was in her grave, a wretched pettifogging lawyer from the purlieus of Deptford, had produced a will of recent date (made, in fact, as soon as Mrs. Brown was aware that she was suffering from the cancer which caused her death) by which all her property, real and personal, was left to her daughter Agatha. It had been Mrs. Brown's one exceptional action in life (corresponding to that one of Agatha's whose results they were just discussing) and had been undoubtedly inspired by the desire to render Agatha free of that dependence upon mankind which even Victorian ladies found so exasperating on occasions. Dad and the boys, as soon as they had recovered from their astonishment, had tried to laugh the matter off. Dad had gone on collecting the weekly rents of the six houses in Beaconsfield Terrace as usual, and as usual had devoted them to his own purposes without rendering account. But those houses were Agatha's all the same, as was the hundred pounds a year clear which they brought in. Will and Harry and Mr. Brown looked at each other with an uneasy suspicion of defeat.

"I'm not a beggar," said Agatha, "so I *can* be a chooser if I like. And I'm going to choose. I'm going to live with my boy wherever I like. So there!"

Will did not know when he was beaten, and he tried to continue the argument.

"Don't be a fool, Aggie," he said, "you can't do that. You can't manage property and—and—have a baby and all that sort of thing. You'll be cheated right and left and you'll come whining back to us for help before the year's out. And then——"

His tone and expression made it unpleasantly clear what would happen then. Agatha only shrugged her shoulders and turned away; she sniffed with contempt as if she had been fourteen instead of twenty-nine and a budding mother. And that sniff completed Will's exasperation. He boiled over with rage at being thus contemptuously treated by a mere woman—and especially at the thought of all that goodly money being taken out of the family.

"Come here!" he said, and sprang across and seized her wrist.

For a second or two the brother and sister stood and glared at each other. But Agatha rallied all her waning moral strength, and continued her amazing rebellion against the godlike male.

"Let me go!" she said.

She tore herself free, and shrank aside from his renewed attempt to grab hold of her. She evaded his grip, and forgetful of all decorum she brought her hand round in a full swing so that it landed with an echoing slap upon Will's pudgy cheek. He staggered back with his ear singing and his heart appalled at this frightful rebellion. Then Agatha turned away and walked slowly from the room, and slowly upstairs to her bedroom, where, with calm, unthinking deliberation she packed the suit-case which had accompanied her on that wonderful trip to London nearly three months before. She included her jewel case with her few petty pieces of jewellery; then, struck by a sudden thought, she opened it again, took out the wedding-ring Samarez had bought her, and slipped it on to the third finger of her left hand. Then, suit-case in hand, she descended the stairs and walked slowly to the front door. The dining-room stood half open as she passed it, and her glance within showed her Dad huddled spiritlessly in his arm-chair, and Will and Harry collapsed and despondent in two chairs by the table. Perhaps if George, her favourite brother, had been there too, Agatha might even then have stayed her steps. But he had not yet returned from work, and the others hardly looked up as she went by. She opened the door and walked out down the pretentious, tiny carriage drive to the road, and turned to the left towards the station. Somehow as she walked thither panic came over her and she hastened her steps more and more until she was almost running. When she reached the station and found there was no up train for half an hour she could not bring herself to wait; instead she boarded the down train and travelled on it for a couple of stations, and then changed trains and returned back through Greenwich.

And so Harry and George, sent out to make peace at any price by a despairing Dad ten minutes after she had left the house, quite missed her.

CHAPTER V

SO that at midsummer, 1893, a pleasant-faced widow, Mrs. Agatha Brown, attired in all the hideous panoply of mourning for a newly-dead husband which the Queen's example had made nearly compulsory, came to live in lodgings at Peckham. Her sympathetic landlady soon knew all about her—about the husband (rather a bad lot, seemingly) who had been in the greengrocery trade and had died suddenly of some rather vague disease, but leaving his widow well provided for by the standards of that simple place and time; about the happy event which was to be expected shortly; about her general friendlessness and the dislike with which her late husband's family regarded her for intercepting the legacies they had come to look upon as their due. Mrs. Rodgers became a great admirer of Mrs. Brown. Mrs. Brown was so evidently a lady, yet withal she had so sound a knowledge of practical affairs, and, most important, she had round her that tremendous aura of "independent means" which implies so much to a working-class dependent for its daily bread upon the whim of an employer. Mrs. Brown paid splendidly regular money for her furnished rooms, but she paid only a tiny amount more than the lowest market value, so that contempt could not creep in to adulterate Mrs. Rodgers's admiration. Mrs. Brown knew all about the prices of things and how long they ought to last, and she always knew how much of her little joints and of her butter and tea and other supplies she had left, so that Mrs. Rodgers's first tentative stealings were calmly checked, and she bore no ill will—quite the contrary. She was soon a very subservient ally.

Mr. Deane, too, who had drawn up that astonishing will of Agatha's mother which had enabled Agatha to become Mrs. Brown of Peckham, was very helpful and kind. He shook his head sympathetically when Agatha, calling upon him, told him about family trouble which had led her to leave home, and of course, seeing that such was his business, he readily consented to take upon himself the management of Agatha's "estate" — the six houses of Beaconsfield Terrace. He looked up curiously and sharply when Agatha explained that at her new address she was known as Mrs. Brown, and when he noticed the expression on her face he pulled his white whiskers and looked down at his notes again in embarrassed fashion. After all, he was a solicitor, and solicitors should not be shocked at encountering family skeletons.

Colchester Street, Peckham, was a brief road of a hundred houses a side, nearly similar but not quite, the pavements grimly flagged, the rest grimly macadamized. At one end was the main road, along which poured a volume of traffic considered large for those times—horse trams and horses buses predominating—and at the other end was a public house, the "Colchester Arms"; but despite this latter handicap Colchester Street was very respectable and at that time very few of the houses accommodated more that one family. Just here and there widows or widowers or maiden-ladies (school-teachers) occupied one or two rooms, but that was a very different matter from other possible developments. Agatha had drifted to 37 Colchester Road as a result of a brief examination of the small advertisements of the local paper; it was the first address she had called at, and she was satisfied. She settled in, and settled down, to a life which was an odd blend of the strictly orderly and logical and nightmarishly fantastic. It was quite orderly and logical of course that she should pay her weekly bills promptly and keep a close eye on her expenditure and exact respect from those whom she encountered, but it was wildly fantastic that she should have no exacting daily duties, that time should hang idly on her hands, that she should have no calls to make nor callers to receive, that she should be addressed as "Mrs.," that she should go to the local doctor and surrender her sweet private body to him for examination and decision on her condition.

The doctor's verdict, of course, was only in agreement with her own. He, too, looked at her sharply; he knew her for a widow and a new-comer, and he guessed shrewdly that there was more in her history than she was likely to tell him, although—although—her sedate costume and sedate, assured manner and placid purity of expression made him doubt his doubts, only to have them return in renewed strength when he found that she was friendly with no woman—that, seemingly, she was without a friend in the world. But he did all his duty and more; he prescribed a regimen for her, gave her information on points of which she was quite ignorant, and finally obtained for her two or three books, written in the genteel round-the-corner style in which such books were then written, which more or less gave her guidance towards the approaching great event.

In the nineties expectant mothers were real invalids; they must not do this and they must not do that, and it were better if they did not do the other; the books hedged in Agatha with all sorts of restrictions and prescriptions, and they took it for granted that she would be really unwell, whereas, if the truth must be told, she never felt better in her life. At times she was puzzled about it, but she took the written word for Gospel—that and the manifold hints and suggestions of Mrs. Rodgers—because, after all, she knew no more about it than what they told her. So now she rose late, only when the children were passing whistling to each other under her bedroom window on their way to school, and she breakfasted in her dressing-gown, and she sat by a closed window (with a fire until summer was indubitably come) and watched the petty pageant of the streets while she stitched and stitched and dreamed and dreamed in all the unreality of occupied idleness.

For, although the books assumed her to be an invalid, they offered some compensation at least in the array of garments they prescribed as necessary for the "little stranger"—that horrible expression of which they made such free use. It was not a horrible expression to Agatha; she would have called it a genteel necessary circumlocution if it had ever occurred to her to employ such an exotic phrase. The "little stranger," then, had to have a myriad garments—binders yards and yards long, matinee jackets, veils and shawls and christening gowns, socks and gloves, day-gowns and night-gowns of flannel exquisitely embroidered in silk—and Agatha made every blessed thing herself, stitching away patiently by the window. She stitched and stitched, but of the dreams she wove in with the silk it would not be right to tell.

She came to know that side street and its habitués so well. There were rag-and-bone men, each chanting his call in his own particular manner; there were the milkmen on the eleven o'clock round, and the smart baker's cart, and the butcher's dog-cart drawn by a showy chestnut sadly overdriven by the butcher's greasy-haired son; there was the insurance agent, frock-coated and bowler-hatted, and the fruit-sellers and knife grinders. On three afternoons a week organ grinders came, one of them with a shivering monkey in a red coat, and another, who was a real Italian, bronzed and handsome with marvellously white teeth, who sang "O Sole Mio" so sentimentally that Agatha always opened the window and threw him a penny. And besides all these there were the children—oh, the children! Every house had its two and three, who came trotting home to dinner at twelve and back again to school at two, and down the street once more at half-past four. Agatha knew them all, the big ones and the little ones, the late ones and the early ones, the good ones and the naughty ones. Big sisters often had one or two to escort, and more than once during those six months Agatha watched the rise of a new independence when some baby boy would suddenly decide that big sisters were no longer of use to him and would find his own way to school, not quite sure of himself either, with an occasional look round to see that the sister was not unattainably out of reach. Agatha could not have watched with greater interest the beginning of a new planet.

Some there were to whom the grim flagstones of the pavement were friendly and sociable, for it was a great game to walk to school entirely on the lines between them; and just outside No. 37 there were three successive very wide flagstones, much wider than the ordinary six-year-old could stride, and Agatha would find herself leaning forward in great excitement to see whether this little boy or that little girl would accomplish the perilous passage in safety. There were naughty little boys who played "knocking down ginger"—knocking at nearly every door in the street and running away before they opened. Agatha's heart used to beat quite fast in case they were caught, but they never were. Tops were all the rage when Agatha first came to No. 37, and they were succeeded by marbles and skipping ropes (according to sex), and cherry stones and little balls and one or two cricket bats made their appearance before football came into its own again. There was one dreadful incident when a prized tennis ball rolled down a drain, and Agatha watched palpitating while the grating was prised up and two small urchins of seven hung on to the legs of another small urchin of nine while he lowered three-quarters of himself head downwards down the hole and reached the ball by a convulsive stretching which threatened every moment to precipitate him upside down into the horrible hole.

It was the little boys in whom Agatha took most interest, although the little girls claimed a good share. She knew the tidy ones and the untidy ones, and the prim ones and the tomboyish ones, and, with typical partiality, she liked the tidy ones best. Her heart was really wrung with agony when a disaster occurred to the primmest and tidiest of them all, when that self-satisfied, smug ten-year-old found her drawers slipping down there in the road with a whole lot of people about. It was into the front garden of No. 37 that she retired, and Agatha, with yearning sympathy, watched her putting matters right while cowering behind the stunted privet bushes.

Strange that children should thus hold her fascinated. Agatha had never before thought about children; she had been too preoccupied with two maids and a house to look after, and the little she had known about the method of arrival selected by children had displeased her. She had felt a sort of contempt for the shapeless, helpless wives upon whom she had sometimes called—Mr. Brown's fellow-Nonconformists were prolific fathers—and she despised wailing babies, and wet babies, and sick babies. All the babies she knew fell into one of these three categories, and children were always quarrelsome, or stupid, or self-assertive. It was all different now; Agatha, stitching a thousand tucks into one ridiculous night-gown, or implanting wonderful embroidery into the corners of a flannel day-gown, thought of few things besides children.

But then of course she was a prisoner for the time, and prisoners, by common report, take interest in spiders and mice and things like that just as Agatha did.

There was one other matter in which she took an interest, though. One day while casually glancing through the newspaper a name caught her eye, and with a slight sense of shock she looked again. The name was that of Lieutenant-Commander R. E. S. Saville-Samarez, and it occurred half-way down a little list headed "Naval Appointments." Agatha may perhaps have seen that column before, but it had conveyed nothing to her. She had not realized before that by its aid she would be able to follow Samarez's professional career, and the discovery stimulated her attention. She found there was another column which sometimes appeared, headed "Movements of H.M. Ships," and with the aid of these two she could trace Samarez hither and thither wherever the Lords of Admiralty might send him. After that Agatha always bought her own newspaper instead of depending on casual readings of Mrs. Rodgers's, and it was for these items that she always looked first. It became her hobby, just as children had become her main interest.

Day passed after day, and week after week. The chair by the first-floor front window had become a second nature to her, just as had her evening walks by side streets. It had almost begun to seem as if she had done nothing else all her life than await the arrival of the son she so confidently expected, and as if she would do nothing else. It called for quite an effort to make herself realize that her time was at hand. Doctor Walters of course treated the affair in a far more matter-of-fact manner, and it was the business-like solemnity of his visits which did most to impress Agatha with the need to complete her arrangements.

Within the last few weeks a new portent had appeared in Salisbury Road, next to Colchester Road. A board had spread itself with wide-open welcoming arms there, bearing the legend "Nursing Home—Surgical, General, Maternity." Until that era nursing homes in the suburbs had been almost non-existent. Suburban people, if they were very ill, went into hospitals; if they were only not quite so ill they struggled back to life or on to death in their own rabbit hutches of houses; nine hundred and ninety-nine suburban babies out of a thousand were born in the suburban beds which had seen their engendering. The average wife would never have dreamed of going cold-bloodedly elsewhere for her confinement, especially when domestic servants were still common. Suburban nursing homes and restaurants and all the other insidious wreckers of home life were only to burgeon into full blossom with the lack of domestic servants. The Salisbury Nursing Home was a little before its time; its "Surgical" and "General" departments were merely heroic gestures, and even its "Maternity" side never flourished. The venture came to a disastrous end after a year's struggle, but that year saw the arrival of Agatha's child.

Agatha made her arrangements with Doctor Walters's full approval, for the doctor, with lingering happy memories of hospital experience and trained assistance and proper appliances, was thoroughly dissatisfied with the makeshifts he usually had to employ in practice, with curtained rooms and feather beds and all the other hideously unhygienic arrangements with which mothers could find no fault. So it was with a strange excited feeling that one day Agatha walked round to the Salisbury Nursing Home with Mrs. Rodgers at her side, carrying the historic suit-case, the suit-case which was accompanying her for the third successive occasion on a great adventure. Agatha liked it all; she liked the bare, clean rooms and the trim, efficient nurses and the cheerfully unsympathetic aspect of the place; for Agatha was of a Spartan turn of mind mostly.

She looked on pain as a necessary part of life; she had been imbued since childhood with notions about "the curse of Eve" and similar predestinate ideas; she knew (and it tortured her) that she had "sinned," and she went unshrinkingly forward. The grit that had carried her father from errand running to wholesaling took her into maternity without a tremor or a regret. The slight pains came, and she was packed away into bed; Doctor Walters called, was unhesitatingly cheerful, and went away again. And then the real pains came, wave after wave of them, so that she found herself flung into a sea of pain of an intensity she had not believed possible. The smooth, efficient face of the nurse, and Doctor Walters's, with its kindly detachment, floated into her consciousness and out again through a grey mist. She caught a whiff of ether, but at the time she had no idea that it was being used on her. Then it was all over (Agatha, looking back, would have said that it had only taken half an hour or so) and she was free to hold her child on her arm for a few wonderful minutes. The delights of motherhood were very obvious and none the less pleasant. It was a boy of course. Agatha had been quite certain of it from the first. Nothing else could have been possible. Agatha to her dying day never realized that it was only a successful even chance, and not a fixed, settled certainty.

CHAPTER VI

SHE called him Albert; goodness knows why. She would not have "Dick," which one might have thought her natural choice. Somewhere within her she realized that Richard Saville-Samarez did not possess quite as much brains as she would like her child to have, and she would take no chances. She had hesitated over "George," but had put it aside in case she ever encountered her family again, for "George" was her father's name as well as her favourite brother's, and she would not have them think that the child was called after them; for it might give them a feeling of proprietary interest, and she did not want that; Albert was all her own. So she chose "Albert." She knew personally no one of that name at all, which satisfied her jealous desire for possession, while about the name there clung a flavour of association with the Royal Family which endeared it to her rather bourgeois little heart.

And Albert Brown grew up and developed just as other babies did, although Agatha would have indignantly denied any similarity. He took his food manfully. He played with his toys at first with the feeble, fumbling fingers of helpless babyhood, and later with the more purposeful action of growing muscle sense. He cut his teeth and fretted over them just as much as one would expect of a healthy child of healthy parents. He achieved his first sitting up and his first straggling attempt to kick. Once or twice he allowed his digestion to become upset. Soon he achieved the miracle of an erect attitude, and eventually came the glorious day when he first addressed Agatha as "Mummy," and not long after that Mrs. Rodgers developed into Miss Ozzes.

For Agatha had returned to No. 37 Colchester Road from the Salisbury Nursing Home. It was comfortable and she did not want to seek out a new resting-place, and Mrs. Rodgers had found no new satisfactory tenant, and—those six months of approaching motherhood had endeared even that unromantic, unambitious little street to Agatha. Moreover, Agatha soon began to establish a business connection in the locality. Albert's marvellous garments were the admiration of all who saw them, and the tale of them was told round about. It was not long before Agatha received tentative inquiries as to whether she would mind making similar things for other Peckham babies, newly arrived or expected shortly. Agatha had found that even the labour of looking after the finest baby in England left her with much free time, and idleness was abhorrent to her. She accepted commissions eagerly, and it was not long before she found that she had little spare time left; those firm, decisive fingers of hers were busy most of the day (when they were not occupied by Albert Brown) stitching away at marvellous embroidery on pelisses and christening robes and, by a natural extension, on wedding dresses and trousseau underclothing. There was not much profit to be made, but still there was a little, and Agatha, although she had found that it was easy enough to live on a hundred pounds a year, was eager to increase her income and accumulate savings. Mr. Deane, the solicitor, had looked at her incredulously when she had told him it was her intention to make Albert an officer in the Navy; he had even hinted as tactfully as he might that perhaps admission to the *Britannia* might not easily be obtained for the illegitimate son of a greengrocer's daughter, and he had declaimed in his soft-spoken way at the expense as a waste of money, but Agatha cherished the ambition none the less. If foresight and money and good training could gain the King's commission for Albert, she was going to leave no stone unturned to provide that foresight and money and good training. Agatha set her round chin firmer still and bent to her sewing with renewed forcefulness.

So Albert Brown grew up in a world of many sections. Upstairs there was his mother, who spoke to him softly and clearly, and whom he knew by continual experience it was best to obey promptly. On the other hand, he knew that if he could manage the perilous descent of the stairs there would be a warm welcome for him from Mrs. Rodgers, who was always ready with a word, or a piece of bread and butter covered with brown sugar, or an unimaginative although ready part in whatever game he chose to devise, or some other equally welcome contribution to his routine. Yet Mrs. Rodgers, with all her honeyed or brown-sugared endearments, did not bulk one half as large in Albert's imagination, and most certainly not in his affection, as did his mother, who played games really well, and who read entrancing books to him, and whose voice, with its sweetness and purity of intonation, was worth a thousand times as much as Mrs. Rodgers's hoarse utterance. Outside the house there was the Street with its myriad mighty attractions—the carts with their big, straining horses, mightily feathered about the fetlocks, hugely hoofed and grandly quartered, hides glistening and nosebags tossing; and errand boys and sweeps and buses and road-mending gangs, and toyshop windows and little boys and girls; and beyond the Street was the Park, where little boys with a high internal pressure of energy could run madly up and down and hoot and screech and scream and look at the boats on the pond and make friends with stray dogs and gallop back to where

Mother was sitting and gallop away again at a gait alternating between that consonant with a horseman in a hurry and a locomotive with its whistle in full blast. The Park and the Street and Upstairs and Downstairs were all exceedingly splendid places most times, and if the earth-rending unhappiness of childhood ever got a grip on you then there was always Mother's sweet-scented breast on which to pour out your woes, and Mother's soft, round arms to go round you, and her nice hands to pat you on the back until your sorrows were inconsequently forgotten. Soon the world had a fifth quarter, which was School, presided over by an omnipotent deity called Miss Farrow, who knew everything, and who was so supremely great that you never realized her smiles might be intended for you, and who on terrible occasions wielded the cane with dreadful results upon such small boys as dared to be naughty. That cane was much more to be feared than any possible smacking Mother might give.

In fact, Agatha, watching the development of her child with all the terrible detachment of a mother born to be gushingly affectionate and restrained by a hot ambition, came early to the conclusion that her son was not a genius, not greatly above the average in brains, and much more amenable to discipline than ever she could picture Nelson or Drake to be in their childhood. He was an orderly and law-abiding sprig of modern civilization; school rules and home rules meant something to him unless the temptation to break them was of an unusually compelling nature. Agatha felt a little twinge of disappointment; surely a child so lawlessly conceived ought to be vastly different from the ordinary herd! But those plans, so often revised and lovingly re-revised during the six months at Colchester Road before Albert's arrival, were easily capable of covering even this state of affairs. The calm foresight of a woman with only herself and her child to consider began to plan a new system of training aimed at carrying young Albert's footsteps with security along the thorny road of Admiralty.

Perhaps if Albert's father had been a stockbroker Agatha's thoughts would have been directed towards stocks and shares. If he had been an artist Agatha would have begun to study art; as it was the fact that he was an officer in the Royal Navy gave her the first necessary impetus towards adopting the Navy as her hobby. The beginnings were small of course—it is not often that we are so fortunate as to be able to trace eventual vast enterprises from their earliest germ—but they blossomed speedily, and their fruit is recorded in the pages of history. Chance showed her how to study Naval appointments and movements in the newspapers; and chance settled the matter by guiding her to the Navy List in the Free Library, where she could study the whole commissioned personnel of the Navy and watch the weary climb of Lieutenant-Commander R. E. S. Saville-Samarez up the heights of Seniority with the ogre of the age limit continually in pursuit. From this it was but a step to those books of reference which described every fighting ship in the world, and in which she could study each successive ship to which Samarez was appointed. It was not long before Agatha had quite a developed knowledge of armaments and tonnages and displacements. She could read about protective decks without bewilderment; she could even follow arguments on the burning question of "Should Armoured Cruisers take their Place in the Line?" It was an extraordinary hobby for a woman to take up; but no one ever dare predict in what direction a woman cut off and isolated from the world will expend her energies. The Library found all sorts of books on its shelves to interest Agatha; she had no use for fiction of course, as became her upbringing, and she read Lives of various admirals, and Naval Histories, and the "Letters of Lord Nelson." If essay writing had been in her line she could have written quite a fair essay on Howe's Tactics on the First of June, or on Nelson's refusal in defiance of orders to expose Sicily. Innumerable references in the books led her on to the study of Mahan and his classic studies of Sea Power, and from thence she was lured inevitably to deep and solemn consideration of the immense sombre influence of maritime supremacy, of the doctrine of the Fleet in Being, and other things which other people do not think twice about. With pathetic cunning she early began to lead young Albert's thoughts in the same direction. If Albert had no genius, then orderly training and astute education of taste might serve the same purpose.

Mr. Deane, the solicitor, could not understand it. He pulled his patriarchal whiskers and stroked his domed forehead, sorely puzzled by Agatha's repeated demands that he should ascertain for her the conditions of entry on the *Britannia*, and the costs of a naval education and similar highfalutin absurdities. He ventured to point out that if Agatha persisted in her decision to send young Albert to the Navy she could count him lost to her from the age of twelve. Agatha fully realized it already, and set her jaw as she told him so. Agatha believed that self-sacrifice was the primary duty of mankind; that man (and much more so woman) was born to sorrow; and that she should give up her child seemed to her right and proper, especially if the Navy benefited. The British Navy was to her the noblest creation in the world; it was the outward and visible manifestation of the majesty of God. Mr. Deane sighed incredulously and impatiently; he had been brought up in a world where women never had any ideas of their own and never,

never dreamed of acting contrary to masculine advice.

Perhaps it was this impatience of his which impelled him along the steep and slippery road on which his footsteps were even then straying. Perhaps he could not bear to see good money wasted on sending Albert Brown to the *Britannia*, and he embezzled it as the only method of prevention. Joking apart, Agatha's insistence must really be taken into account in estimating the circumstances of the misdeeds of that venerable old hypocrite.

Temptation certainly came his way. A whole series of road improvements and tramway extensions and industrial developments in South-East London had led to the sale of a great deal of house property lately—Agatha's included. Mr. Deane found himself in charge temporarily of a large amount of his clients' capital. Mr. Deane—the awful truth appeared later—led two lives, one in the company of his good wife, and the other in the company of a damsel of a class which the newspapers sometimes designated as "fair Cyprians." Mr. Deane's expenses were naturally in excess of his income. Mr. Deane endeavoured to right such a state of affairs by tactful speculation. Mr. Deane selected the South African market as the field of his activities. Mr. Deane lost money, for South African securities slumped heavily before the threat of the South African War. Mr. Deane shrank from the thought of suicide, or of prison and poverty. Mr. Deane gathered together what remained of his clients' negotiable assets and departed for Callao, accompanied by the fair Cyprian. The Official Receiver found much work to do in clearing up the ruin left by Mr. Deane.

Agatha's money had nearly all vanished. The Official Receiver sorted out for her a tiny fraction of the original capital, but it was a woefully small amount. The fate which Will Brown had predicted for her money had descended upon it. It was that fact, that prophecy of Will's, quite as much as anything else, which made Agatha set her lips and turn with energy into continuing her life's work without reference to the family. She would not go back to them, nor crave their help. She would not have them say, "I told you so." The fine sewing which she had done light-heartedly before to earn luxuries now was called upon to supply necessities. Lucky it was that she had built up a connection, and that not much further effort was needed to establish herself in the good graces of the local big drapers and gain herself a small but assured market. No *Britannia* for Albert now. If she had thought her father or her brothers would have supplied the money for that she would have gone back to them and eaten humble pie, eaten the bread of penitence and drunk the waters of affliction, but she was all too sure that they would not. Their idea of their duty towards her would include the necessity of boarding Albert out and getting rid of him, to the colonies or the mercantile marine, as rapidly, inconspicuously and inexpensively as possible. They were heathens, infidels, upon whom the light of the Navy had not descended.

So fine sewing, embroidery, pleating and button-making continued to earn the daily bread of Agatha and Albert. One more set of plans had to be devised for Albert's future. If he was not to receive a commission in the usual way (perhaps it was as well that Mr. Deane had been involved with the fair Cyprian, for

Albert might easily never have made his way past a Selection Board) then he must gain one in the unusual way. Commissions sometimes were gained by the lower deck—" aft through the hawsehole " was the technical expression. Albert must begin as a seaman and work his way upward. If he started with sound ideas on his profession, with enthusiasm—fanaticism—and a good general education, it might well come about. Agatha kept her two hundred pounds in the bank against that day, when he would need an outfit and some money to spend, and flung herself with ardour into the business of providing Albert with the grounding she thought necessary.

That was easy enough, for Albert was an amenable little boy, and he had not nearly enough personality (it would have been extraordinary if he had) to withstand the infection of all Agatha's enthusiasm. A board school education was of course all his mother could afford for him, but a board school education backed up by strong home influence will do as much for any boy up to eleven years of age as any other form of education. Agatha had been taught at a young ladies' college, but her sound common sense and mighty will enabled her to recover from this catastrophe. So that even while Agatha was entering upon the study of the higher aspects of Sea Power and gaining a blurred insight into the ballistics of big gunnery she was at the same time helping Albert with his sums and beginning his first tentative introduction to Drake and Nelson.

Tentative indeed, for Agatha found it impossible to bestow upon Albert the high dramatic insight which infused her dreams. Ships were just ships to young Albert. He could not picture them, as Agatha did, as minute fragments of man-made matter afloat on an enormous expanse of water, smaller relatively than grains of dust upon a tennis lawn, which yet could preserve, positively and certainly, an island from a continent. Albert could not be impressed (perhaps it was more than could ever be expected of a ten-year-old) by the mighty pageant of England's naval history. Lagos and Quiberon, the Nile and Trafalgar were to him mere affairs where Englishmen asserted their natural superiority over Frenchmen; their enormous consequences, both hidden and dramatic, were to him inconceivable. He was a matter-of-fact young man, and Agatha dully realized the fact, with vague disappointment. Even Agatha, with all her dreams and insight, could not foresee the sprouting of the grain she was sowing in such seemingly inhospitable soil.

CHAPTER VII

WITH the birth of her child Agatha suddenly entered upon a wonderful late blooming, like the blossoming of an autumn rose. She put on a little more flesh—but flesh in the 1890's was in no way the abomination it was to become in later years. When Agatha walked nowadays she gave hints of broad, motherly hips and ample, comfortable thighs beneath her skirt, and her arms were very, very plump and round, and her face had filled out smoothly and deliciously, accentuating the creaminess of her really lovely complexion. She was a fine Junoesque woman now, stately, queenly even, and her stateliness was borne out by the dignified placidity of her facial expression. She was a mother to be proud of—a mother, especially, to admire; small wonder, then, that young Albert was strongly influenced by her ideas and never dreamed of acting contrary to them.

Little Mr. Gold loved her at first sight. He was a nice refined little gentlemanly man, whose name was most eminently appropriate, for he had hair of pale gold (not as much, now, alas, as he once had had) and gold-rimmed spectacles, and across his insignificant little stomach was a gold watch-chain with a gold medal. He was neat in his dress and precise in his habits, and when one was once able to overlook the faintly receding chin and the general lack of personality about his face he was quite a handsome little fellow; it was a pity that all his character had been refined right away. Mr. Gold in conversation often made great play with remarks about "leading boys instead of driving them" and "kindliness always tells in the long run," and this, it is to be feared, were outward signs of an inward timidity, for Mr. Gold was a master at an elementary school—at the school Albert attended, in fact. Mr. Gold, when he was taking a class, would often make a great show of anger; he would shake his fists and try to make his eyes (little pale blue eyes) flash fire, and he flattered himself that by so doing he was successful in intimidating the boys, but Mr. Gold never entered into conflict of personality with boys singly, never caned one, lout of fourteen or child of eight, without feeling an inward tremor of doubt—"What on earth shall I do if he won't hold out his hand when I tell him?" Mr. Gold had even developed the weakest characteristic of a master; he would send big riotous boys to the headmaster for quite minor offences, dodging a personal clash under the voiced explanation that they had done something much too wicked for him to deal with.

All this, though, was quite lost on young Albert when he was moved up from the infants' school and entered Mr. Gold's class in the boys' school. If Mr. Gold had any effect at all upon Albert, it was a slight impression of neatness and dapperness; Albert had too great a respect for authority to dream that it might ever be possible for a master to have limbs of water and a heart of fear. And when, one evening, just after school, Albert fell down in the playground and cut his chin rather badly, Albert was quite grateful to Mr. Gold for the kindly manner in which he washed the cut and staunched the bleeding and inquired how he was feeling now; and finally Albert took it quite kindly that Mr. Gold should walk down Colchester Road with him in case he should feel ill on the way, and to explain to his mother that the bloodstains on his shirt and collar were not really his fault.

It was of course tea-time when Mr. Gold and Albert reached No. 37 Colchester Road; the china gleamed upon the tablecloth and the kettle steamed beside the fire. What could be more natural than that Mr. Gold should be asked to have a cup? And nothing could be more natural than that Mr. Gold, landlady-ridden bachelor that he was, should yearn for the comfort of Mrs. Brown's sitting-room and fireside, and should accept with alacrity—alacrity which warmed into well-being when Mr. Gold began to notice Mrs. Brown's beautiful complexion and well-filled bodice.

Young Albert, of course, as soon as the novelty of having a schoolmaster to tea wore off, found the situation irksome and quietly made his way out of the room, but Mr. Gold lingered. He expanded in the grateful warmth of the fire and Agatha's well-trained deference towards the superior sex. They chatted amicably enough for quite awhile before at last Mr. Gold took himself off after having begged permission to come again, and Agatha at his departure found herself almost dreamy. Queenly she was, but she was of that type of queen which inclines towards a Prince Consort. Mr. Gold's personified inadequacy made a very definite appeal to her. Why, he was almost shorter than her; she could pick him up and carry him if she wanted to. And he was so refined and gentlemanly too (as a matter of fact, "refaned" was the most frequent word on his lips), while he avoided being so terrifyingly of the public school class as Commander Saville-Samarez. Agatha actually began to calculate what effect a marriage with Mr. Gold might have upon her cherished ambition for Albert, and she decided it would be a good one.

And of course, Agatha having decided that, Mr. Gold's career as a bachelor was as good as ended. Not that he was unwilling; he walked away from No. 37 through the dusky side streets with his mind full of rosy visions. Mr. Gold was not at all a man to think often about arms and legs, and certainly not about the other parts of the female body, but he caught himself doing so quite often that evening. The hang of the back of Agatha's skirt, and her neat hands, and her sweet face and firm bosom all conspired to set him imagining. Next morning in class he treated Albert with such downright favouritism that Albert's fellow nine-year-olds turned and rent him at playtime.

But one single moment of expansion sufficed to destroy all Mr. Gold's chances. The pity of it was that he was never to know what it was which snatched from his reach all Agatha's sweet charms, which deprived him of the encirclement of her round white arms, which barred him for ever from the paradise of her breast and the calm sweetness of her throat. It was at Mr. Gold's third visit, or it may have been his fourth—it was his last, at any rate. Mr. Gold was sitting by the fire in the single arm-chair; he was comfortably inflated with tea and hot buttered toast and an extraordinary good opinion of himself; all three combined to bulge out his waistcoat.

Agatha, of course, as an inferior female ought to do, was sitting before the fire on a less comfortable chair, bent over her sewing. The charming femininity of the pose made a vast appeal to Mr. Gold; he admired the bent head and neck with the firelight playing upon them; whiteness and roundness combined to set little pink pictures moving at the back of his mind. He even visualized Agatha's legs in their trim stockings—and of course, as the old vulgar saying has it, there was something in her stocking besides her leg! Agatha *and* a bit of money; an efficient housekeeper and a white-armed wife! The picture was far too irresistible. Mr. Gold puffed himself out a little more; soon he would propose, and he would taste the honeyed sweetness of those demure lips. Meanwhile, the present line of conversation was pleasant; he continued it, laying down the law to the accompaniment of Agatha's dutiful "Really ?s" and "Of courses."

Agatha too, as she sewed, had little pictures, only not nearly as defined, at the back of her mind. Not, of course, that she visualized any normally clothed portion whatever of Mr. Gold's anatomy. Agatha did not have that sort of imagination. But she had vague ideas of feeling Mr. Gold's weak little face pressing upon her breast, and of clasping him in her arms, and of spending every evening as a wife should in the less comfortable of the two chairs by the fire while a tired husband told her what she ought to think about the world in general. But she suddenly stopped sewing, aghast, when the import of Mr. Gold's latest remarks penetrated to her active intelligence.

"And all this money we spend on unproductive things too," Mr. Gold was saying. "I don't believe in it. A one-and-sixpenny income tax will ruin the country before very long Look at the money we spend on the Army and the Navy. Millions. This *Dreadnought* that they speak about. Twelve-inch guns and all. To my mind it's only an excuse for spending money so that there will be more places for people's nephews and cousins. What do we want a Navy *for?* Who's going to attack us, and what good would they get by it, and what harm would it do, anyway? A Navy doesn't do any good to anyone except the people who get good jobs in it. Germany's getting just as bad, apparently. It's all a lot of silly dangerous nonsense. Look at the last war. What right had we got it South Africa? None at all. We were wrong to fight, and it was the hotheads who forced us into it. I said so all along, although of course it made me unpopular. That was why I had to change my school and come to Colchester Road. They called me a pro-Boer, and all that sort of thing. But I stuck it out. I'm a man of peace, I am."

Mr. Gold only ceased when he noticed the look on Agatha's face. That so alarmed him that he got up from his chair.

"Good gracious, Mrs. Brown, whatever's the matter? Are you unwell?"

"No," said Agatha, shrinking away from him. "No."

She was merely appalled by the heresies she had heard enunciated. That Mr. Gold, whom she thought she liked, should be a Little Englander, an advocate of disarmament, a pro-Boer, a scoffer at the *Dreadnought!* It was far too terrible for words. At the same moment she realized what a terribly narrow escape she had had. She dreaded to think what the result upon Albert might have been had he had Mr. Gold as a stepfather. Fancy a world without a British Navy! It was dreadful. Mr. Gold, try as he would, could have thought of nothing to say that could have hurt her more.

"No," said Agatha. "I'm quite well."

Quite unconsciously she was imitating the heroines of the novels she had read in the dead old days before the British Navy took hold of her. She "drew herself up to her full height," her eyes "flashed fire," she "made an imperious gesture."

"Please——" said Mr. Gold.

"I—I think it is time for you to go," said Agatha.

Poor Mr. Gold simply could not understand it.

"But, Mrs. Brown——"

All Agatha did was to walk across the room and open the door, and it would have taken some one of stronger personality than Mr. Gold to have withstood the implied command. He crept out crest-fallen, and Agatha shut the parlour door decisively behind him. Nothing remained for Mr. Gold to do except to take his hat and coat from the pegs on the landing, stumble downstairs, and let himself out.

"Now listen, Mrs. Rodgers," said Agatha that evening, "if that—that man ever comes again, tell him I'm not at home. You understand?"

And she looked so queenly and her eyes flashed so bright as she said it that Mrs. Rodgers could only say "Lor, mum, yes, mum," and gaze at her with admiration and without a thought of asking questions. Moreover, when Mr. Gold, inevitably, came calling again, she conveyed Agatha's message to him with such force and unction as simply to infuriate the unfortunate little man. He had written to her already, and Agatha had simply ignored his letter. He made up for it in the end by calling Albert out of class and giving him a good hiding for no reason whatever.

When Albert told his mother about it later Agatha merely nodded and offered no consolation. She did not mind at all if antipathy sprang up between Albert and the heretical Mr. Gold.

Quite on the contrary. Besides, Agatha knew, without even Albert telling her, that hidings from Mr. Gold were not of much account.

Mr. Gold eventually solaced his puzzled exasperation by convincing himself that Agatha was mad.

CHAPTER VIII

SO years followed years, and each succeeding year dragged more heavily and painfully than did the one before. To Agatha's tortured conscience it seemed as if retribution was being exacted from her for her vile sin. To her it was natural that a lifetime of pain and squalor should be the consequence of a five days' madness. Fine sewing sank steadily in value; private customers fell away—the economic causes of a falling birth rate and marriage rate broke her on their wheel. There was not so much demand nowadays for baby clothes or wedding dresses, and simplicity was creeping into fashion even in such garments as were ordered of her. The shops which had first bought her output had grown larger and had amalgamated, and obscurely she was squeezed out from supplying them. Competition was growing fiercer, and money was scarcer in the 1900's than it had been in the 1890's. Agatha's earnings grew smaller, and there were often weeks when she had to draw upon her hoarded capital to meet Mrs. Rodgers's weekly bill. She was finding less work and smaller pay for what she did.

Nor was this all. Physical pain, that last exaction by a relentless deity in payment for her sin, had come into her life. Sometimes it was slight, and Agatha could seemingly set it aside unnoticed. But at other times it was sharper, more intense, drastic. It was not a fair pain. It did not come upon her when she was expecting it and braced against it. When she stood up from her chair and held herself ready for it it did not come, but the instant she relaxed to go on with what she was doing it fell upon her and rent her with agony. It was a fierce, horrible pain.

It had begun to come upon her when Albert was eleven, when he had grown into a thick-set freckled boy with unruly hair just like his father's. He had done more than his masters had expected of him by winning a scholarship and proceeding from the Council School to a secondary school. Agatha's careful supervision of his studies thus bore its first fruit. She was maternally proud of his progress even while she had to reconcile herself to the fact that he was only an ordinary little boy—just like what his father must have been. Agatha, with a growing obsession of sin, tried hard not to think of Albert's father, but Albert reminded her of him at every turn, overwhelming her with conscience-stricken yearning for something unknown—certainly not for further contact with the Commander, even though she had followed his progress step by step up the Navy List, and had watched apprehensively the reports of the combined expedition in China in 1900 (wherein Commander Saville-Samarez had led a portion of the Naval Brigade), and had even prayed that he would not be damagingly involved in the great Fisher-Beresford feud which was then threatening the Navy with disruption.

Agatha still was up to date in naval affairs. She followed all the twists and turns of the controversy between Lord Charles and Sir John; she appreciated the trend of new construction so that the details of the *Dreadnought*, when they were published, roused no surprise in her; she thoroughly understood the import of Fisher's new policy at the Admiralty whereby ships were scrapped in scores and the Navy recalled to home waters until nine of its guns out of ten were pointing at Germany.

But all that, of course, was before pain came upon her. Pain, and the pressing need of seeking more and more work, began to distract her from this life study. She tried to accept the pain in the philosophic spirit with which she had accepted all the other buffetings of Fate. Pain was all a woman should expect, especially a woman who had sinned as grievously and unrepentantly as she. Pain was natural to a woman at her time of life. Pain—the grinding, lacerating spasms of agony brought sweat down her drawn face and made her gasp and choke even as she was trying to explain it to herself. She lost her smooth, placid good looks. Her cheeks fell inwards and her mouth compressed itself into a harder line. Wrinkles came between her eyebrows as a result of the continual distortion of her forehead during the agonizing bursts of pain.

Young Albert, full of the pressing and immediate interests of a new school, and a secondary school at that, did not notice the gradual change which came over his mother—nor is it specially surprising, seeing that Agatha always managed to raise a smile for him on his entrance, and continued, with a fervour more vivid than ever, to impress upon him the great tradition of Duty and the magnificence of England upon the seas, rousing his limited imagination to heights one would have thought unscalable to such a combination of the solemn and matter-of-fact. He did not even notice at first his mother's unaccountable fits of sudden abstraction and convulsive gripping of the arms of her chair.

But there came a time when even Agatha could no longer endure her torment, nor explain it to herself as natural in a woman of forty-three. For the second time in her life she yielded up her body to Doctor Walters's anxious examination, and for the second time listened to his verdict. A different verdict this time, delivered sadly instead of jovially, with regret instead of hope. Even as he spoke Agatha realized that what he was saying was not news to her—it only voiced a fact she had refused to admit to herself. Doctor Walters's heart was wrung with pity, as only a heart can be upon which pity makes continual demands, the while he told her what he had found, told her of the operation which would be necessary—and strove to keep from his voice any hint of what he knew would be the end even after the operation. Agatha looked him in the face as he spoke; she was not of the stuff that flinches. It was Doctor Walters instead who avoided a meeting of the eyes. He was sick at heart the while he chafed to himself about the cursed suffering obstinacy of womankind which postpones action until action is too late.

So Albert came home from school to a new world, a world where Mrs. Rodgers had to deputize for a mother who had vanished, her place preposterously taken by a shattered wreck in the hospital, moaning vaguely and turning dim, unseeing eyes upon him. He went on at school in the unimaginative fashion which was to be expected, but now his Wednesday afternoons and Saturday afternoons were spent in journeys to the hospital and in a few fleeting, worried minutes in a chair beside his mother's bed.

She died hard, died game, as befitted the daughter of a self-made man. She rallied round despite the fearful things they did to her with knives. For a little while the authorities even began to think that she would make a recovery, unexpected and nearly inconceivable. For a little while understanding returned to her, and she was able to smile upon the scared little boy at her bedside and talk to him sensibly about his work—and his future. That future! There was one afternoon when she stretched her arm out suddenly from the bedclothes (a frightening arm; pain and suffering had stripped the smooth flesh from it and left it a skinny bundle of bones and tendons) and pointed it at him.

"Albert," she said, "Albert, you know about the Navy? You know you're going to join the Navy?"

"Of course, mother," said Albert. That had been understood between them for years now.

"Promise me, then, boy," said Agatha. Her eyes were too large for her thin face, and she gazed at him with an intensity which scared him.

"Of course I will, mother. Of course."

Agatha's scarecrow hand dropped, and she

turned aside her face contentedly again, much to Albert's relief.

But before ever she had begun to regain strength the cancer which had gnawed at her lifted up its foul head again. There was a significant shaking of heads among the hospital staff. Next time Albert came he found a feebler, stranger mother still. She did not know him. Her eyelids were drooped until the line of pupil they still allowed to show appeared inhuman and unnatural. She was inert and dreamy. Opium had her; the doctors were kind. She would die the pleasant death of the poppy, and not that of the lunatic torture of cancer. Each succeeding visit of Albert's found her muttering and silly. Towards the end pain reasserted itself. Opium began to lose its mastery, and little stabs of agony showed themselves on her face, and a surprised ejaculation or two broke through her mutterings. Yet Fate was kind enough; Agatha's life went out of her while she floated above a vast grey sea sombrely tinted with opium, while around her loomed up the immense beetling silhouettes of the battle squadrons, the grey, craggy citadels of England's glory and hope. Their funnel smoke swirled round her, veiling the worried freckled face of the child of her sin, and she smiled happily. Mrs. Rodgers wept hysterically on Albert's shoulder.

For Mrs. Rodgers had gloried vicariously in Agatha's illness. It was of the right savoury type to appeal to her. It was something to talk about with pride to her friends, with much whispering of gory and distorted detail; it was a disease from which only women could suffer, and hence a source of immense interest. 'Orse-pitals and operations and cancer of the womb—why, they provided her with precedence in conversation for months afterwards. She had, naturally, full charge of the funeral arrangements subsequently too, and that was unmixed delight. There was a hundred pounds in Agatha's account at the bank, so that Mrs. Rodgers had no need whatever to skimp or scrape about it. Agatha could have a funeral worthy of the lady she was. She could have the best oak coffin, and a first-class 'earse, and 'eaps and 'eaps of flowers—Mrs. Rodgers bought two or three wreaths out of Agatha's money, because of course Agatha had not known enough people for their contributions to make a good enough show—and two coaches. Mrs. Rodgers was able to ask all her intimate cronies too, and indulge in all the orgy of ghoulish formality for which her soul craved. Albert had to have a black suit, and a black tie, and black gloves—Mrs. Rodgers would have insisted on a black shirt too if there had been any shadow of precedent for it—and travel in the first coach as chief mourner along with Mrs. Rodgers and Mr. Dickens, the vicar, and two of Mrs. Rodgers's best friends. And there were mutes in plenty, in tall hats and frock-coats, walking with solemn, dignified sorrow beside the hearse. And when the business was over there was a real slap-up dinner at No. 37, with cold 'am and tongue and beef and trifle and port and sherry, with afterwards cup after cup of strong tea and delightful conversation around the fire with half a dozen women with their best party manners and black gowns. Quite one of the happiest and most satisfactory days in all Mrs. Rodgers's life. Albert went through it all in a waking nightmare, and afterwards remembered hardly anything about it.

CHAPTER IX

THERE is little enough need to lay emphasis on the next section of Albert Brown's career. Aged fourteen and a half, he could not join the Navy (as he knew already) until he was fifteen and a quarter. Mrs. Rodgers fussed over him until even he, insensitive though he was, could hardly bear the sight of her He said good-bye to his school with hardly a twinge of regret; he had early been impregnated with Agatha's fatalistic tendencies and he could, even at fourteen, accept the inevitable without complaint. Totally without introspection and without much notice for the circumstances in which he found himself, he was never more than vaguely unhappy during the following nine months.

He had the sense to keep to himself his crystallized determination to join the Navy as soon as he was old enough—he never said very much at any time—and the school sympathetically found him an office boy's position with a City firm. The only part of his life that he really hated was the bowler hat which convention compelled him to wear—even Albert could appreciate the hideous incongruity of a bowler hat on a fourteen-year-old head—and it was not until afterwards that he realized how much he detested everything connected with an office boy's life. He left home (he called Mrs. Rodgers's house "home" still) at ten minutes to eight each morning, and he came back at half-past six each night. He travelled on a tram to Blackfriars from Camberwell Green and to Camberwell Green from Blackfriars. He swept out the front office, he filled ink-wells, he took messages (painfully learning his way about London in the process); he brought in cups of tea from the teashop next door (this was, of course, before the era of regular office teas); he copied letters; he was slightly initiated into the beginnings of book-keeping; he experienced the incredible boredom and occasional fierce spasms of work which every one in an office experiences. And since ordinary diligence was habitual to him, and honesty was part of his mental content, and he had brains of a quite good average order, he was looked upon with approving eyes by the powers that were, and after six months his wages were raised from five shillings a week to seven and sixpence. This official recognition gave him no thrill of pride or pleasure; office life was a mere marking time before he took the tremendous stride towards the goal he not merely desired, but considered necessary and inevitable. The time came at length for him to take it.

When Albert Brown was fifteen years and three months old all but one week he approached the chief clerk and gave him the week's notice which the law demanded. The chief clerk looked Albert up and down and whistled softly in surprise. He remembered painful experiences with other office boys, Albert's predecessors, who were one and all slack and unpunctual and dishonest and given to lying and who were intolerable nuisances to every one. He contemplated with dismay a renewal of these experiences and all the bothersome inconveniences of having to train another boy. He realized that stock-taking, the quarterly upheaval, was nearly due, and that Albert's absence would be really tiresome.

"What in hell do you want to leave for?" he demanded. "Or are you just playing up for another rise?"

"Don't want a rise," said Albert. "I only want to give notice."

"Got another job, I suppose?" said the chief clerk.

"No," said Albert.

"Well, you *are* a looney," decided the chief clerk. "You're getting on well here. In another six months—or any day, in fact—you'll be junior clerk here. Look at *me*. I was junior clerk here, once. What in the name of Jesus do you want to give notice for? Had a fortune left you?"

"No," said Albert.

"Well, what are you going to *do*, then?"

"I'm going to join the Navy," said Albert.

"Whe-e-e-ew," said the chief clerk; he was certain now that Albert was crazy.

The office entirely agreed with him. Only

boys who were suffering from an overdose of penny dreadfuls would ever dream of leaving the sequestered calm of an office for the uncertain turbulence of a fighting service—and they would not do more than dream of it. As for acting upon the dream, throwing up a safe job for a trifling whim, that was sheer lunacy. The Junior Partner himself saw fit to emerge from his Olympian seclusion and to discuss the matter with this extraordinary office boy; there were almost tears in his eyes as he besought Albert to reconsider his decision; in the end he utterly broke down—broke down far enough, at any rate, to offer Albert yet another half-crown a week on to his princely salary if only he would stay on and not blast his career in this fashion. But even this mighty condescension and this magnificent temptation left Albert unmoved. He hardly noticed them, although the storm of incredulous astonishment his announcement raised (quite unexpectedly to him, for he considered it the most logical move possible to join the Navy at fifteen and a quarter) left him slightly bewildered. He persisted in giving notice. In the end the Junior Partner yielded.

He patted Albert on the shoulder, and swallowed hard, and produced some second-hand platitudes about the Navy—" wish more people had as much interest in the Navy "—" very healthy and natural for a boy to want to join "—" Nelson "—" England expects "—" hope you do well, my boy." Then finally, and most extraordinary of all, he fished three half-crowns out of his pocket, gave them to Albert as his next week's wages, and told him he could leave now and have a week's holiday before taking the decisive step. For which ridiculous proceeding he was heartily cursed (privately) by the outer office, which he had heedlessly left office-boy-less, the while he earned no gratitude whatever from Albert, who did not find any joy in a week spent hanging disconsolately about unnecessarily exposed to the maudlin pleadings of Mrs. Rodgers, who wept profusely over him at every opportunity, and who took it for granted that entry into the Navy implied an immediate watery grave.

Authority at Whitehall, when Albert presented himself, received him with open arms. This was the kind of stuff they needed for the Navy—

an orphan without a relation in the world, and no half-starved weakling either, but a sturdy, well-set-up young man of undoubted physique. Educated too; three years at a secondary school, nine months in a City office, with the very best of characters from both. Written characters were not much in evidence with most of the stray candidates for admission to the Navy. Boys from good homes who joined at fifteen as a result of a vocation were either the best of material or woefully bad bargains, and Albert had all the earmarks of the good material. Albert's birth certificate (Agatha, fifteen years ago, had rendered herself, unknowingly, liable to imprisonment on account of a false declaration to the registrar) was duly inspected and passed. He had no legal guardian (Albert indignantly denied Mrs. Rodgers's claim to that position) and no next-of-kin. That was all quite uninteresting; the Navy of course did not know (neither did Albert) that Albert Brown was the only son of Captain Richard E. S. Saville-Samarez, C.B., M.V.O., nor that through his paternal grandmother he had two second cousins in the peerage.

Yet, however it was, Albert was a man of mark after six months at Shotley Barracks. His was not an original mind, Heaven knows, and he was not of distinguished personality. But a secondary school education which had gone as far as the beginnings of trigonometry and mechanics was not common at Shotley. And he was not an institution boy, nor was he the starveling scion of a poor family either. The institutions which supplied a great part of the young entry were admirable affairs for the most part. They fed and clothed and even taught the waifs who drifted into them quite adequately, but no institution can help being an institution. The boys who came from them all displayed, unavoidably, some signs of being machine made. Independence of thought or action, careless assumption of responsibility, spontaneous action—all these are, inevitably, foreign to the boy who has spent all his life in a regular routine under close adult supervision in narrow contact with hundreds of his fellows. Albert, on the other hand, had the natural self-containedness of the only child; he was accustomed to independent and solitary action; even those hated months in the City office had served their turn in broadening his mind and accustoming him to keeping his head in encounters with strangers. His memory was good even though his brains were not brilliant, and little of the hard-earned knowledge gained at school had faded out during his City life. The very elementary mathematics taught at Shotley were child's play to him even while they were stumbling blocks to his misty-minded fellows. The severely practical instruction in seamanship was a joy to his logical mind, and his fingers were deft in their work and powerful when strength was demanded. Albert's main competitors, in fact, were never the institution boys, but the sons of seamen—petty officers' sons destined to follow in their fathers' footsteps, dockyard artificers' sons, and boys from coast towns, in all of whom the tradition of the sea was strongly imbued, and who had in most cases the same sort of advantage over Albert in seamanship as he had over them in theoretical work. But to most of these boys rules and regulations were a sad stumbling block. Breaches of discipline were unhappily habitual among them, thanks to their exuberant high spirits and independent intolerance of control. For them was the cane, the extra lesson, the awful terror of the Commandant's wrath. Good young Albert, who found discipline merely a convenient means to an end, knew nothing of these frightful penalties. His record sheets remained unstained by the black blots they bore in their train. Albert's career moved logically and inexorably onwards through musketry and swimming and elementary gunnery and seamanship and drill, from second-class boyhood to first-class boyhood, from Shotley Barracks to H.M. Training Ship *Ganges*, until at last even first-class boyhood was left behind and he became a full-blown ordinary seaman in the newly commissioned third-class cruiser *Charybdis*, which left Portsmouth late in 1912 to continue the old tradition (sadly weakened by new strategical arrangements) of showing the Flag in Eastern waters and to maintain the very necessary policing of those rather disorderly shores.

Albert Brown was not, let it be repeated, of an imaginative or romantic turn of mind. It is doubtful if he experienced any of the conventional thoughts as England vanished from sight, or if emotion of any sort came to him Quite likely he was feeling annoyed about the lower-deck crowding resulting from the fact that *Charybdis* was taking out drafts on board for other ships on Eastern stations ; conceivably there passed through his mind some vague wonderings about promotion ; but his last glimpse of England (the last of all his short life, as it turned out) meant nothing more to him. His intense love for his country, his delight and pride in her naval might, his glory in her past and his ambitions for her future, were real enough and solid enough ; they were a living and essential part of him. But they found no voice. Brown had no use for words in relation to them, and they were too deep to raise any surface disturbance, any facile emotion. Brown turned solidly to his duty the while the relentiess thrust of *Charybdis*' screws bore him away from the land for which he was ready to give his life.

CHAPTER X

THE beginning of the war found *Charybdis* at Singapore. There was a buzz of joy throughout the lower deck; even among the ratings of the Navy the opinion had grown stronger and stronger that Germany's huge naval effort could only end in war between England and Germany, and for years now the English sailor had forgotten the centuries-old blood feud with France and had awaited with joyous expectation the North Sea clash, in anticipation of which he had been steadily withdrawn from the Mediterranean and the Pacific by the foresight of his supreme controllers, so that at the very time when England's Navy was stronger than ever it had been there was a smaller English force than ever before in Eastern waters. And that summer night when the First Fleet, happily mobilized, went speeding northwards to its gloomy war station at Scapa, the

· preparative" flashed by wireless and cable to the few scattered units which flew the White Ensign in the Pacific.

For there was cause for some anxiety there. Von Spee was lost in the vast expanse of the ocean; he had cannily cleared from Tsing-tao before ever the war clouds had grown over ominous, and no one knew where he might appear or when he might strike. His armoured cruisers, *Gneisenau* and *Scharnhorst*, held the big gun records of the German fleet, and what that meant was all too clear to the minds of those who had gained an insight into the achievements of German naval gunnery. There were light cruisers with him too; whether others had joined him since his departure from Tsing-tao was not known for certain—Muller with the *Emden* and von Lutz with the *Ziethen* were free to attach themselves to him if they wished—but it was obvious enough that he had a fast-moving, hard-hitting squadron which any English fleet without battleships might without shame be chary of encountering. No one knew where he might appear; he could strike at the South American nitrate trade, at the Indian shipping, at the South African coast where were Boer rebels and German armies to welcome him; on the high seas there were fleets bearing Australian troops, New Zealand troops, Indian troops, English troops. If one such fleet were left unconvoyed he might encounter it and deal one of the most terrible blows given in war. At every point of danger there had to be stationed against him a squadron of strength superior to his own, and England was, as ever at the outbreak of war, woefully short of cruisers. The naval might of England had definitely asserted its superiority—the German merchant flag had vanished from the seas with the outbreak of war, and the German battle fleet had withdrawn in sullen impotence to the protection of its minefields—but here in the Pacific there was this one rebel, hopeless and desperate, who might yet strike a fierce blow or two before Fate overtook him.

That in the end Fate would overtake him there was no doubt whatever. With the Japanese declaration of war and siege of Tsing-tao he had no harbour left him. Coal could only be obtained with difficulty through German agents established here and there before the war. The myriad spare parts he would need would be unobtainable; the myriad small defects which would develop would be irremediable. His ships' bottoms would grow foul, and there was no graving dock open to him. Sooner or later, whether or not he encountered an enemy, he would have to call the game lost and seek internment in some neutral port. But were he not hunted down and destroyed the material damage he might do would be enormous, and the damage to British prestige would be more serious still. Small wonder that the air was electric with messages flying back and forth summoning all the scattered Pacific units of the British fleet into rallying groups converging on the million square miles wherein he lay concealed.

The lower deck ratings of *Charybdis* thought nothing of the task. They put a happy trust in their officers, who would bring a superior force against von Spee; and if they were not in superior force, then English grit and English gunnery would take no heed of odds and would carry the matter through just as at Trafalgar or the Nile. No man aboard *Charybdis* but would cheerfully and eagerly have accepted the chance to fight in that obsolescent cruiser against *Scharnhorst* or *Gneisenau* with their deadly 8-inch guns. They eagerly anticipated victory; it is only giving them their due to say further that they would have gone as willingly to certain defeat for the Navy's sake. For the terrible superiority of the 5.9 over the almost obsolete Mark IV. 4.7 they cared nothing. The lower-deck buzz was cheerful and vigorous, and the knowledge that the war-heads were being set in the torpedoes was sufficient compensation for the hateful fatigue of hurried coaling.

Leading Seaman Albert Brown (he had been Leading Seaman now for a fortnight after a bare year as Ordinary Seaman, and another as A.B.) had a more intimate knowledge of the facts and probabilities. He knew, as did the others, of the imminent hunt for von Spee, but he had a clearer appreciation of the difficulties. The *Charybdis* could not hope to fight successfully any one of the majority of von Spee's squadron, and she had hardly speed sufficient to escape danger. *Scharnhorst* or *Gneisenau*, those big armoured cruisers, would blow her out of the water instantly. *Ziethen*, an earlier and smaller armoured cruiser, would have hardly more difficulty. Brown even foresaw serious danger in an encounter with a light cruiser, with *Emden* or *Dresden*, with their smaller but more modern and dangerous guns. But Brown had the better kind of courage; he could foresee danger and not flinch, not even inwardly. If death came to him—well, he died, and that was the end of speculation. If not—war-time and an expanding Navy meant promotion. He was Leading Seaman now, though barely twenty. The commission he hardly dared to think about seemed at last a faint possibility instead of an incredible possibility. Brown knew that it was the first step in promotion which was the hardest to come by.

So *Charybdis* left Singapore hurriedly and drove eastward, obedient to the flickering wireless, into the widespread deserts of the Pacific. This was the very earliest beginning of the war, before Japan had turned against Germany and sent her army to Kiao-chau, and her navy in a wide sweep south-eastwards after von Spee. *Charybdis* took her course across the China Sea;

she nosed her way through the Carolines, exploring that straggling group of flat, miserable islands, and from the Carolines she threaded her way through dangerous seas on to the Marshalls. On the opposite side of the world an anxious Admiralty awaited her reports, for the Carolines and Marshalls were German possessions, and there, if anywhere, would von Spee be found. But a thousand miles of sea leaves much room in which a small squadron can be lost, and *Charybdis* missed contact with von Spee by the barest margin of twenty-four hours. *Charybdis'* negative reports, relayed round the world, came in to puzzle the naval staff more than ever. They were at a loss to think where von Spee could have hidden himself. The Australian navy was on its guard to the southward; the Japanese fleet was sweeping down from the north; a concentration was gradually taking shape at the Falklands. There was a loosely-knit combination forming against von Spee, but there was room enough for him to slip through if he cared to. Reports were instantly to hand that Muller, in *Emden*, had indeed slipped through; she was at large in the Indian Ocean, ravaging the rich merchant shipping, capturing and sinking and destroying. She had stolen in disguise within range of Madras, and had shelled the invaluable oil tanks there. But her movements were no indication of von Spee's whereabouts, for he had clearly detached her and moved in some new direction himself—perhaps right across the Pacific. Contact with him must be made. He might even pass the Panama Canal and appear in the West Indies, and break across the Atlantic in a desperate effort to reach home. The wireless orders summoned *Charybdis* farther yet across the Pacific, south again to the Line to a secret coaling station and onwards towards Panama, with every nerve strained awaiting the look-out's report that von Spee was in sight—a signal to set the wireless transmission crackling, proclaiming his presence to all the world, the while the helm brought the ship round in desperate flight from those deadly 8-inch guns.

Blind chance—the chance that had ordained von Spee should evade *Charybdis* in the Marshalls, and which sent him to his death at the Falklands —directed that here, in the most desolate waters of the world, cruiser should meet cruiser. Von Spee, striking across to the South American coast, had detached *Ziethen* (Captain von Lutz) with orders to steer for Australasian waters. *Ziethen*, with her large displacement, her ten 6-inch guns and thick armour, would be a match for any of the British light cruisers; against her the British would have to scatter broadcast armoured cruisers, and that implied an absence of defence against the blow he meditated against the Falklands. *Ziethen*, being in no way homogeneous with his own squadron, could be well spared. So *Ziethen* was detached, and a thousand miles from land she encountered *Charybdis*.

Charybdis saw a smudge of smoke on the horizon. *Charybdis* steered towards it. Soon *Ziethen's* three tall funnels could be descried. The Captain of *Charybdis* peered anxiously through his glasses. He ran through his memory to pick out which remembered silhouette was hers.

"That's *Ziethen*," said Captain Holt. "Now, where are the others?"

For a few minutes both ships held on slightly divergent courses, each anxious to ascertain whether the other was in the company of others. But no other smoke clouds showed upon the horizon. They were alone upon a waste of water.

"Fight or run?" said the Captain to himself, knowing the answer as he said it.

Run? He must not run. It was his duty to shadow *Ziethen* if he could not fight her, keep her under observation by virtue of his half-knot superiority of speed until some one came up who could fight her. But shadow a ship of superior force over two thousand miles of dangerous sea with only such a tiny additional speed? The odds would be a hundred to one that he would lose her—and his professional reputation along with her. Leading Seaman Albert Brown, gunlayer of No. 2 4.7 gun, at his action station, paralleled his Captain's thoughts as they occurred. He must fight then—old 4.7's against new 5.9's, four thousand tons against eight thousand. Luck might aid him; a sea fight is always a chancy business. At the worst he might do *Ziethen* some serious damage before *Charybdis* sank, and the *Ziethen* seriously damaged meant the *Ziethen* rendered useless, for she had no place where she might effect repairs.

"Action stations" had gone long ago; steam was being raised in all boilers; the propellers were beating a faster rhythm as both ships tried to work up to full speed, swinging round each other in the momentary sparring before rushing in to grapple. The Captain put the glasses to his eyes again, and while he did so, casually, as befitted an Englishman at a mighty crisis, he spoke to the man at the wheel. Round went the wheel, and *Charybdis* heeled as she swung round sharply under maximum helm at high speed. The Captain was making the most of his chances, closing the range as rapidly as possible to avoid as much as he could being hit without being able to hit back. Even as *Charybdis* came round the wireless signalman was sending out, over and over again, the message telling of the encounter, giving latitude and longitude, trying to inform the expectant British fleet where *Ziethen* was to be found. And while he did so *Ziethen's* operator was "jamming" hard. No message could hope to get through that tangled confusion, especially over a distance of thousands of miles, in the unkindly ether of the Pacific.

But *Ziethen* was ready for *Charybdis'* manœuvre. Well did Captain Lutz appreciate the superiority of the 6-inch over the 4.7. He put his helm over too, and *Ziethen* came round until the courses of the two ships were almost parallel, and, as *Charybdis* turned further, he continued his turn until it almost seemed as if he were running away. It was a pretty sight, those two great ships wheeling round each other on the blue, blue Pacific with a blue sky over them and peace all about them. Only the spread smudges from the heavily smoking funnels marred the picture.

"Out of range still, curse them!" groaned the Gunnery Lieutenant, hearkening to the monotonous chant of the range-taking petty officer.

A sudden little haze became apparent round *Ziethen*, and almost simultaneously a group of tall pillars of water shot up suddenly from the surface of the sea two hundred yards from *Charybdis'* bow. The Gunnery Lieutenant started in surprise. Practice as good as this was more than he expected. *Charybdis* heeled again under pressure of helm in her effort to close. The tall fountains of water shot up again, this time only a hundred yards from the quarter; some of the water splashed on to *Charybdis'* deck. The thunder of *Ziethen's* guns did not reach her until half a dozen seconds later.

"Bracketed, by God!" said the Gunnery Lieutenant, and then, in surprised admiration of a worthy opponent, "Good shooting! Dam' good shooting!"

Charybdis turned sharply to disconcert the German range takers, but the next salvo pitched close alongside, flooding the decks with water. Down below, below the level of the water, under the protective deck, the stokers were labouring like lunatics to supply the steam which was being demanded so insistently; but *Ziethen's* stokers were labouring too, and proof of their efforts was displayed in the huge volumes of smoke pouring from her funnels. Victory might well incline to the ship which first reached her maximum speed; speed would enable *Charybdis* to close, or enable *Ziethen* to keep away and continue to blast her enemy with salvoes to which no reply was possible. Once only did the Gunnery Lieutenant see his beloved guns in action; once only. They fired at extreme range, on the upward roll, but it was a vain hope. The Gunnery Lieutenant groaned his bitter disappointment—the more bitter because the hope had been so frail—when he saw the tall columns of water leap half a mile on the hither side of the enemy. But the anguish of the Gunnery Lieutenant's soul ended with his groan, for *Ziethen's* next salvo, flickering down from the blue, came crashing fair and deadly upon the *Charybdis'* deck; five 6-inch shells falling together. They blew the Gunnery Lieutenant into bloody and unrecognizable rags; they dashed to pieces the range-taking petty officer and his instrument; they wiped out the crew of No. 4 gun; they left the superstructure riddled and the funnels tottering; they started a blaze of fire here, there and everywhere, so that the Executive Officer and his hose-party, choking in the smoke, could not cope with one-half of the work before them. Nor was that one salvo all. Salvo followed salvo, with barely half a minute between them. The pitiless shells rained down upon the wretched ship, smashing and rending and destroying. The *Ziethen's* gunners were toiling with the disciplined rapidity resulting from years of gun drill, heaving up the heavy hundred-pound shells and thrusting them home with a trained convulsive effort, training, firing, reloading, not even, thanks to their solid discipline, sparing a moment to view the ruin they were causing. *Charybdis* reeled beneath the blows; smoke poured from her in increasing volume, but her vitals, her motive power, were down below her protective deck, and she could still grind through the water with undiminished speed. The Captain was down and dying, torn open by a splinter, and it was the Commander who gave the orders now; dead men lay round the guns, and the stewards were bearing many wounded down below to where the Surgeon laboured in semi-darkness; but scratch crews manned the guns, which flamed and thundered at hopelessly long range. Yet fierce resolution, half a knot more speed and a slightly converging course all did their work. The high-tossed pillars of water crept nearer to *Ziethen*, and soon a shrill cheer from a gun-layer, cutting through the insane din, greeted *Charybdis'* first hit. There were dead Germans now upon *Ziethen's* deck.

But *Charybdis* was a dying ship, even though the thrust of her screws still drove her madly through the water. Her side was torn open; she would have been wrapped in flame were it not that the shells pitching close alongside sometimes threw tons of water on board and extinguished some of the fire. The merciless shells had riven and wrenched her frail upper works until the dead there outnumbered the living. Her guns still spoke spasmodically through the smoke; the White Ensign still flew overhead, challenging the interloping Black Cross on a white ground which flaunted itself from *Ziethen*. When the oldest navy met the newest pride left no room for surrender; barbaric victory or barbaric death were the only chances open to the iron men in their iron ships. Feebly spoke *Charybdis'* guns, and for every single shell which was flung at *Ziethen* a full salvo came winging back, five shells at a time, directed by an uninjured central control, with the range known to a yard. Even as *Charybdis* made her last hit her death was in the air. It smote her hard upon her injured side; it reached and detonated the starboard magazine so that a crashing explosion tore the ship across. The hungry sea boiled in; the stokers and the artificers and the engineers whom the explosion had not killed died in their scores as the water trapped them below decks. Even as the boilers exploded, even as the ship drove madly below the surface, *Ziethen's* last salvo smote her and burst amid the chaos caused by its predecessors. In thirty seconds *Charybdis* had passed from a living thing to a dead, from a fighting ship to a twisted tangle of iron falling through the sunlit upper waters of the Pacific down into the freezing darkness of the unfathomed bottom. Above her the circling whirlpools lived their scanty minute amid the vast bubbles which came boiling up to the surface; a smear of oil and coal dust marred the azure beauty of the Pacific, and at its centre floated a little gathering of wreckage, human and inhuman, living and dead—nearly all dead.

CHAPTER XI

THE record of Brown's doings while *Charybdis* fought *Ziethen* is not material to this history. He was only a part of a whole, and whatever he did the credit belongs not to him, but to the Navy, the tremendous institution which had trained him and disciplined him. If in the last few desperate moments he fought his gun without superior direction, that was because handling a 4.7 under all conditions had been grained into his nature; the credit should rather go to the whiskered admirals of an earlier epoch who had laid down the instructions for gun drill. Brown was a brave man, and he did not flinch from his post, but many men less brave than he would have done the same had they been parts of the same whole. It was the Navy of the unrivalled past which gained glory from the defeat of this, an inconsiderable fraction of itself, just as that same Navy must bear the blame, if blame there is. That is as it should be, but at the same time the argument hands over to Brown all the glory and honour for what he did on Resolution, and to Brown as an individual must be given the credit for the eventual destruction of *Ziethen*. For he acted on Resolution without orders, on his own keen initiative, under conditions where neither discipline nor training could help him.

That was all still in the future, however, and not one of the German boat's crew which picked him up as they pulled through the scattered wreckage knew that they would soon meet their deaths through the agency of this shaken fragment of humanity. Very thoroughly did the boat's crew search, rowing hither and yon over the oil-streaked water, but they found little. There were two dead men—one of them so shattered that he hardly appeared human—two or three wounded, and one merely half-stunned; this last was a stoutly-built fellow of medium height, very freckled, with hard grey eyes and light brown hair, inclined to be as rebellious as was possible within the narrow limits of its close crop. He was very badly shaken, having been blown from the deck to the water when the magazine exploded, and he was hardly conscious of holding on to a stray rolled hammock which came to the surface providentially near him when *Charybdis* sank. He lay limp in the bottom of the boat as it rowed back to *Ziethen*, and he had to be assisted to the ship's deck.

All he wanted at that time was to allow his weakness to overcome him, to fall to the deck and sleep heavily, but the exigencies of war would not allow him that luxury. He was the only one of the three survivors of *Charybdis* who was even half conscious, and Captain Lutz, bearing on his shoulders the responsibility for *Ziethen* and her hundreds of men, must know at once how *Charybdis* came to be where she was; whether she had consorts near who could have heard her wireless, whether the meeting was intentional or accidental—everything, in fact, which would enable him to spin out his little hour in being. They did not treat Brown unkindly; they dried him and gave him spirits and wrapped him in a comfortable woollen nightshirt and allowed him to sit in a chair in the dispensary beside the sick-bay while he was being questioned.

Brown rolled dazed eyes over his questioners as he sat huddled in his chair. The bearded officer with the four rings of gold lace must be *Ziethen's* captain, he knew; the young officer was a sub-lieutenant; the shirt-sleeved man was the Surgeon (who had been doing gory work on the half-dozen wounded *Charybdis'* shells had injured), and the naval rating in the background was the sick-bay steward.

Fierce and keen were the Captain's questions, uttered in a guttural and toneless English; occasionally the Captain would turn and speak explosively in German to the Sub-Lieutenant, who in turn would address Brown in an English far purer and without a trace of accent. Brown made halting replies, his eyelids drooping with weairness. He told of *Charybdis'* slow progress through the Carolines and Marshalls, and steady course eastwards across the Pacific. No, he did not know of any other English ship near. He had heard nothing of any concentration against the German squadron. It was at this point that the Captain called upon the Sub-Lieutenant to interpret, and the Sub-Lieutenant duly informed Brown in passionless tones that a prisoner who made false statements was guilty of espionage, and as such was liable to be shot, and undoubtedly in this instance would be shot.

"Yes," said Brown.

Was *Charybdis* expecting to encounter *Ziethen?*

"I don't know," said Brown.

What was her course and destination at the time of meeting?

"I don't know," said Brown.

Now, did he want to be well treated while he was on board?

"Yes," said Brown.

Then let him answer their questions sensibly. Whither was *Charybdis* bound?

"I don't know," said Brown, and at this point the medical officer intervened, and Captain Lutz left him testily. Brown had been speaking the truth when he said he did not know; but he had a very shrewd idea all the same, and had he told Captain Lutz of his suspicions he might have relieved that officer of a great burden of worry. But that was no way Brown's business

—on the contrary. Captain Lutz's ill-timed threat had reminded him of the fact at the very moment when, in his half-dazed condition, he was likely in reply to kindly questioning to have told all he knew or thought.

The Surgeon spoke to the sick-bay steward, who summoned a colleague, and between them they tucked Brown into a cot in the sick-bay, put a hot bottle at his feet (shock had left him cold and weak) and allowed him to fall away into that deep, intense sleep for which his every fibre seemed to be clamouring. And while Brown slept *Ziethen* came round on her heel and headed back eastwards.

For *Charybdis* had not gone to the bottom quite without exacting some compensation. One of her 4.7-inch shells had struck *Ziethen* fair and true a foot above the water-line, and a yard forward of the limits of her armour belt. There the shell had burst, smashing a great hole through which the sea raced in such a volume that the pumps were hard put to it to keep the water from gaining until, after the battle, a sweating work party had got a collision mat over the hole, while inside the stokers cleared the bunker, into which the hole opened, of the coal which interfered with the work of the pumps. Examination of the damage showed it to be extensive. Nowhere else on all the side of the ship could a shell of that calibre have been put to better use. The forward armour plate, starboard side, was slightly buckled and loose on its rivets ; there was a hole in the skin ten feet across, one-third of it below water, and, worst of all, the bulkhead and watertight door between the injured compartment and the next (the boiler compartment, and largest of all) were involved in the damage as well. The ship was actually in danger ; in smooth water she had nothing to fear, but, given a Pacific gale and Pacific rollers, the collision mat inevitably torn off, and the pumps choked with coal-dust, two compartments might fill and *Ziethen* would go to join *Charybdis* on the bottom.

Clearly it meant the postponement of *Ziethen's* projected raid. The New Zealand meat ships and the Australian convoys would be left in peace for the time. No captain would risk his ship on a long voyage in such a condition, least of all the captain of a German warship with no friends within five thousand miles, with the constant possibility of a battle at any moment, and the certainty of one sooner or later. *Ziethen* must find a harbour, a haven of some sort, where she could rest while her shattered hull was being patched, and that without delay. A neutral port would mean almost certain internment, the most ignominious ending possible to a voyage; or if by any miracle she was not interned, her presence would be broadcast far and wide, and on her exit from neutral waters she would find awaiting her an overwhelming force of the enemy. So that ports with docks and stores and necessaries were barred to her. She must find somewhere a deserted piece of land from which news would not spread, where she would be able to find shelter while her own artificers forged and fixed new plates, and where it was unlikely that enemy warships would find her or inquisitive Government officials complain of breaches of neutrality. In the Pacific there was more than one such haven, but the nearest was far superior to all others; Captain Lutz knew the answer to the question he set himself before even he had found it by consultation of charts and sailing directions. Resolution Island, that last, most northerly outlier of the Galapagos Archipelago, would suit him best of all. So *Ziethen* set her course for Resolution Island, a thousand miles away, her pumps at work, while a relay of sweating artificers down in the Stygian depths of her toiled to keep them clear. Brown slept the heavy, exhausting sleep of profound shock the while *Ziethen's* propellers beat their monotonous rhythm, driving her onwards to where Brown's fate awaited him.

He slept all the rest of the day and most of the night. And though he had the sailor's habit of sound sleep and the readiness of sleep of the strong-minded, towards morning he was wakened more than once by a painful, unexplainable noise, a bubbling howl which in his sleepy condition appeared to him to be neither human nor connected with the ship. It died away each time, however, and he slept again, but in the morning, when he was fully awake, he heard it again. It seemed to come from the other side of the bulkhead, and he could not explain it to himself. He looked about him; he was alone, although there was another empty cot in the cabin. The interior was a cool white, and a whirling electric fan helped out the port-holes in their business of ventilation, but the air which came in hardly seemed to cool the cabin. For *Ziethen* was almost on the Equator, and iron decks and iron bulkheads mean a sweltering heat under a vertical sun. The heat was dry and redolent of hot metal, but Brown was used to it; two years on the lower deck in the tropics had made such a state of affairs almost normal to him.

Brown had not much time to think before the sick-bay steward he remembered from yesterday entered the cabin. His jolly German face creased into a smile as he saw Brown normal and conscious again. He put a thermometer into Brown's mouth, and smiled again as he read it and noted the result on the chart at the head of the cot. He spoke to him amicably, and grinned as he realized that Brown did not understand a word he said. He made Brown comfortable as dexterously as a nurse might, twitched the blankets into place and smoothed the bedclothes and waddled away with a friendly look over his shoulder. Ten minutes later he returned with the Surgeon.

"Bedder, eh ?" said that officer with a glance at the chart. Automatically he took Brown's wrist and produced his watch simultaneously, felt his pulse and nodded.

"Any bain any blace ?" he asked.

"No, sir," said Brown.

"Feeling all right, eh ?"

"Yes, sir."

"You gan haf breagfast, den."

The Surgeon spoke to the steward, who vanished and returned almost at once. He brought good grey bread and tinned butter, and coffee which was not as good as either; but Brown relished it all. As the Surgeon retired the steward brought him a bundle of clothes—shirt and jumper and loose trousers, and socks and shoes; they were the white duck uniform of a German sailor, and Brown put them on, a little troubled by the minor differences between it and the English naval uniform—the collar, for example, had to be buttoned awkwardly inside—but the general fit was not too bad. The plump steward still grinned in elephantine friendliness.

The rest of the morning passed. The Commander, cold-eyed and detached, came in on a round of inspection, ran his eye over him and went his way without a word. Then he was led once more into the presence of the Captain and searchingly questioned. Brown did his best not to give information; he fell back when hard-pressed upon a stolid, brainless stupidity, and the most penetrating questions rattled harmlessly from his "I don't knows." And since it was extremely probable that a mere leading seaman from an isolated cruiser should know nothing, the Captain in the end dropped the inquisition. And, after all, it is doubtful if anything Brown could have told him would have added to Captain von Lutz's information. The Captain was about to dismiss him when the Sub-Lieutenant interposed with a respectful question. The Captain thought for a moment, exchanged a few sentences with the Sub-Lieutenant, and uttered his verdict. It was a verdict settling Brown's fate—and the fate of *Ziethen* too, but no one was to know that.

Brown heard of the decision on his return to the sick-bay.

"You are to helb here," said the Surgeon to him.

Brown could only stare without understanding, and the Surgeon (with enormous condescension on the part of an officer towards a man in ordinary seaman's uniform) explained in a fatherly manner.

"What are we to do wit you on board here?" he asked. "Pud you in prison? Prison is not good in the dropigs. You gan ztay and helb nurse your vrients. You will not run away, we know."

And he laughed throatily; Brown did not realize how exceedingly condescending it was on the part even of a non-combatant German officer to crack a joke with a seaman.

It was thus that Brown learned the explanation of the groaning noise of the night before. The plump steward led him into the adjoining ward of the sick-bay. There on two cots lay two wrecks of men. One had his head half swathed in bandages, through which once more a red stain was beginning to show. He lay on his back in the cot with his fingers writhing, and through a shapeless hole in the bandages over his mouth there came a continued low, bubbling groan—low now, but clearly likely to rise at any moment to that higher penetrating pitch Brown remembered so well. Half a forehead and one eye remained uncovered to show Brown that beneath the bandages lay what had once been the homely, friendly features of Ginger Harris, a messmate of his and a bosom friend of two years' standing. There was no hint of recognition in that one eye of Ginger's when it opened; all Ginger's thoughts were at present concentrated upon himself. Later, when Brown saw what was beneath the bandages, he was not surprised.

The second cot was occupied by a leading signalman whom Brown did not know at all well, and he hardly recognized him because of the marble-like pallor which had overspread his face; he was so thin and so exceedingly pale—even his lips were white—that he was more like a soulless visitor from another world as he lay motionless in the cot. Brown wondered what was the injury from which he was suffering, and looked inquiringly at the fat steward. The latter soon enlightened him; he indicated a bulge beneath the bedclothes, whirled his arms round like a windmill, said "Sh-sh," and tapped his leg. Brown grasped his meaning; the leading signalman had come within reach of one of *Charybdis'* gigantic propellers as she sank and had lost his leg. Perhaps he had been lucky in that the whirling blades had not cut him to mincemeat instead of merely hacking off a limb, but Brown realized that there could be two opinions about that.

So that he and these two wrecks were the sole survivors of the four hundred and odd men who had constituted the crew of *Charybdis*. Four hundred dead men were drifting in the middle depths of the Pacific, a prey for the shark and the squid. It had been a vain, frantic sacrifice, part of the price the Navy must pay for the glory of keeping the bellies of an unthinking population charged with their accustomed meat and bread. Brown could picture, back in England, the arrival of the news of the loss of *Charybdis* with all hands. The tea-parties would say, "Dear me, how sad!" and go on talking about cancer of the womb; and the business offices would say, "Mismanagement somewhere, of course," and revert to the Cesarewitch or the delinquencies of office boys. Brown had no illusions about that. He knew how little the people for whom he was fighting appreciated his services and those of his fellows. They might inflate themselves with pride over having the largest Navy in the world, and sing little songs about "Britannia, the Pride of the Ocean," and stand a bluejacket a drink, and the better read might talk hazily about "the command of the sea"; but of the irresistible strength of sea power, of the profundity of study and research and self-sacrifice necessary to employ it—or of what lay beneath Ginger Harris's bandages—they knew nothing. Brown's upper lip rose a little, and his blunt chin came forward at the same time. None of that affected his determination to do his duty; his duty to the Navy, to himself and (although he would not think of it in those words) to the memory of his mother. He would help feed the babbling mob of civilians, if he could, but not for the civilians' sake.

Later he found himself jeering bitterly at himself for his highfalutin determinations. He was a prisoner in the hands of the enemy, and helpless. He could think of no means to hold back *Ziethen* from her mission of destruction. As soon as her side was repaired she would go off capturing and sinking British ships, just as *Emden* was doing. Five million pounds was a small estimate of the cost of her probable sinkings. And he would be forced to witness them—or else, with contemptuous carelessness, he might be put on board a neutral vessel to find his way home while *Ziethen* continued her career. There was nothing he could do. He knew too much about the internal discipline of a ship to hope to disable the engines or bring off any other boy's adventure book coup, although it must be admitted that he tried to think of some scheme to achieve some such end. Helplessness and despair and loneliness combined to force him into frightful despondency—the utter black misery of the twenty-year-old—during the three days that *Ziethen* was ploughing her crippled way to Resolution.

CHAPTER XII

THE Galapagos Archipelago is a group of volcanic islands, bisected by the Equator, seven hundred miles from the American coast. They support no inhabitants—mainly because they have little water—and they are sufficiently distant from the ordinary trade routes (at least until the opening of the Panama Canal) to have remained comparatively unvisited. Their flora and fauna have followed their own lines of evolution without interference from the mainland, so that they boast their own special species of insects and reptiles and cacti. The monstrous Galapagos tortoises gave the Archipelago its collective name, but the individual islands were christened by the Englishmen who called there on sundry occasions—Albemarle, Indefatigable, Chatham, Barrington, Resolution and the rest are all reminiscent of ships or admirals or statesmen. Hither came Woodes

Rogers and Dampier, privateering, and Anson with King George's commission. The Pacific whalers—Hermann Melville among them—called to stock their ships with tortoises. H.M.S. *Beagle* came here a hundred years ago with a young naturalist of an inquiring turn of mind on board, by name Charles Darwin, who was so struck by the evidences of evolution among the living creatures there that his thoughts were directed to the consideration of the Origin of Species by Natural Selection.

Resolution Island is the loneliest and least visited of them all. Once it was a volcanic crater, but it has been extinct for a thousand years or more, and the Pacific has broken in at one point so that in shape it is an incomplete ring of towering cliffs surrounding a central lagoon half a mile across. The entrance gives twenty fathoms of water; the centre of the lagoon is of unplumbed depth. The cliffs themselves (the ring is nowhere more than a quarter of a mile thick) are of lava in huge tumbled jagged blocks with edges like knives, the lower slopes covered thinly with spiky cactus, the upper slopes a naked tangle of rock. The extreme highest ridge, however, where the wind had had full play, has been somewhat weathered down, so that the lava edges have been blunted, and are disguised, by a layer of smaller pumice.

One glimpse of that central lagoon convinced Captain von Lutz that here indeed was the haven he desired. It was a land-locked harbour which would give shelter in any wind that blew, and already in his mind's eye he could see *Ziethen's* side repaired and the ship herself free to traverse the Pacific and wreak confusion and destruction among the helpless British mercantile marine. Cautiously he made his entrance, for the sailing directions are excessively vague regarding Resolution. He sent a picket boat on ahead, and followed her cautiously, sounding as he went. *Ziethen* breasted gallantly the race of the tide through the gap (for at the ebb the piled-up water in the lagoon comes surging out through the narrow exit like a mill-race) made her way through with the naked cliffs close on either hand and emerged safely into the lagoon. As she entered the stifling heat of the place closed in upon her with crushing force, for the cliffs cut off the wind and the sun beats down all day upon their sloping surfaces and is pitilessly reflected inwards to a central focus. But heat must be endured; cautiously and very, very slowly *Ziethen* swung sideways. An anchor roared from her hawsehole and took grip of the bottom away from the vast depths of the central throat of the old crater. Tide and propellers and rudder were balanced against each other while another anchor was got away from the stern, and soon *Ziethen* was riding safely and comfortably in the heart of Resolution. It was a sound piece of seamanship, which Brown thoroughly appreciated, despite the fact that his view of the proceedings was limited to what he could see from portholes.

And as soon as mooring was completed, *Ziethen's* crew sprang into furious action. Alone on a sea where every man's hand was against them, it was dangerous to linger within sight of land however deserted. The work must be done at once, so that *Ziethen* could emerge from her concealment, with sea room to fight if necessary, and her injured side healed, so that she could fight or run or capture as occasion dictated. The stokers were set to work clearing the starboard bunkers as far as might be and transferring their contents to the port side. The Gunnery Lieutenant supervised the activity of a party which laboured to empty the starboard magazines and fill the port ones. Even the starboard battery twelve-pounders were unshipped, with infinite labour, and taken across, and the central guns were trained out to port. For a modern ship in fighting trim is not so easy to careen as were the tiny wooden ships of the buccaneers. To expose a foot of the ship's bottom necessitates the transference of hundreds of tons of weight—and even that is a dangerous and chancy matter in a ship whose sides are plastered with armour plate. Small wonder that *Ziethen* needed the shelter of Resolution for the business.

All this dawned upon Brown as he looked round him during the dog watches that evening when he was allowed upon deck under the friendly chaperonage of the fat steward. He looked up at the towering cliffs, and felt the increasing heel of the deck. If those cliffs were in the possession of an enemy with a gun—a six-inch—a twelve-pounder even! *Ziethen*, heavily listed, would be helpless. Her decks could be swept, the repairing party overside could be wiped out, and the mending of the side could be postponed indefinitely, until either the ship was sunk or she remedied her list again and cleared off in disgust to some new refuge; and refuges as good as Resolution were necessarily amazingly few. He scanned the desolate cliffs again, warily. They were barely more than a quarter of a mile away at any point, within easy rifle-shot, in fact. Rifle-shot! An idea sprang into pulsing life in Brown's brain, and the blood surged hot beneath his skin. He turned away from the fat steward lest he should betray his sudden agitation. But again and again he peered up at the cliffs, turning over in his mind the details of his plan, searching for flaws in it and debating consequences. He could find no flaws; he could foresee possibly profound consequences.

Back in the sick-bay, alone, waiting to hear the feeble cry of the Leading Signalman or the renewed sound of Ginger Harris's agony, he plunged more seriously into his plans. If he could delay *Ziethen's* repairs for a time, or if (as he hardly hoped) he could drive her away unrepaired, he would have achieved much. Somewhere, of course, British ships were seeking her out, and the longer she could be kept in one spot the more chance they would have of finding her. The news of the sinking of *Charybdis* must have brought many ships hot upon the trail. (Brown did not know that *Charybdis*' wireless messages never got through, and the loss of *Charybdis* was at long last ascribed to internal causes, the same as accounted for *Bulwark* and other ships.) To hold *Ziethen* helpless for a few days might well settle the matter. It might cost him his life, but that was a price he expected to pay. Nelson and Blake and Drake had given their lives in other wars. And although a slight tremor ran through him at the thought of dying—death comes hard at twenty—it did not affect his determination at all, or weigh in the balance of his plans. Agatha Brown's influence was bearing its fruit, and perhaps his heritage on the male side from a long line of fighting naval ancestors had something to say in the matter too.

Brown's escape from *Ziethen* was absurdly

simple. This of course was largely because he was not expected to want to escape—who on earth would desire to be marooned on a barren and waterless island?—and partly because at first sight it seemed as if his escape would be a relief for *Ziethen*. Prisoners of war are out of place on a raiding cruiser; to hold them safely means treating them harshly, and no one on board had the least desire to treat Brown harshly. Yet he was definitely in the way where he was, save for the fact that he was of some slight assistance in the nursing of the two English wounded men. He was a bit of grit in the machinery of *Ziethen*—slight, but noticeable.

Now at the foot of the gangway outside the sick-bay stood an arms rack. In the rack stood twelve rifles, and above them hung twelve sets of equipment. For *Ziethen* was a raiding cruiser, and must be ready at a moment's notice to send away an armed boarding or landing party. The rifles and equipment stood ready for the use of one of the boats' crews. Brown had noted them casually more than once, but now he opened the door and stole out gently to examine them more closely. The rifles were heavily greased, as was necessary in the tropics. The equipments were in marching order, ready for instant use. He felt the pouches; they were full—sixty rounds per set. The leather pouches at the back of each belt contained two heavy packages—a day's emergency ration in each. The water-bottles were empty, however. Brown removed two, tiptoed back and filled them, and drove the corks well home. Inside the door he listened carefully, heard no one coming, and slipped out again. He replaced one water-bottle in its sling and buckled the other to the belt of the same set of equipment. He emptied the pouches of another set and filled his pockets with the ammunition. He put another day's rations into the pouch of the set he proposed taking with him, and his preparations were complete. If, with two days' food and water and one hundred and twenty rounds, he could not keep *Ziethen* thoroughly annoyed for a week he would be very surprised.

But to be ready to depart was one thing; to transfer himself and his captures to the mainland of Resolution was quite another. Brown realized how easily his plan might fail at this point, and how discovery would mean an ignominious marching off to the punishment cells and the end of all his hopes. That was a risk that had to be faced, however. He had weighed the chances and had decided he might perhaps succeed. All that was necessary, in fact, was a cool head and moderate good fortune. It would be a distortion of English to say that Brown had a cool head; at the moment he was a mere incarnation of duty, selfless and unselfish and impersonal, so that coolness of head had nothing to do with his condition. He was a fighting machine, and as little likely to become flustered as any other machine.

Outside it was tropically dark; the young moon had not quite cleared the highest ridge of Resolution, to light the lagoon and the ship within. Brown lifted the full set of equipment, put it over his shoulders, and buckled it about him. He took a rifle, slung it on one shoulder, and stole up the gangway. In five seconds he was crouched beneath the port side boat swung in its davits, unobserved by the watch, by the armed sentry, or by any casual wanderers. With noiseless unfumbling rapidity he set about his preparations for the next step.

With his knife he cut the lashings of the boat cover, reached inside and pulled out, after a small search, two of the lifebelts which were there in readiness. One of them he bound about his rifle as tightly as he could; it would be a sorry fiasco if the weapon were to sink and he were to arrive on Resolution safe but unarmed. The other he bound about him. Then he fished out one of the boat's lines and dropped the end very, very quietly overside. Slinging his rifle again, he gripped the rope and lowered himself down. He was hampered by the bulkiness of the lifebelt and the mass of his equipment, but patience and brute strength saved him from swinging with a crash against the steel side of the ship; he went down foot by foot, cautiously. At last he felt the sea at his ankles, and by the time he had reached the end of the rope it was at his waist. He let himself fall the rest of the way, sinking until the water closed over his head in his effort to avoid a splash before the lifebelt brought him to the surface again. The rest was easy. Lying as much on his back as the lifebelt would allow, and clinging like grim death to his rifle, he struck out gently with his feet along the ship's side; the water was as warm as milk. Heading steadily and patiently past *Ziethen's* stern he moved away by almost imperceptible degrees. It was half an hour before his slow, powerful strokes bore him to the side of the lagoon, and he had to swim along the side for another ten minutes before he could discover, in the faint light of the rising moon, a bit of beach which shelved sufficiently to allow him to clamber up. There he unfastened the lifebelts and dropped them in a cactus clump, and hitching his equipment more firmly round his wet body he set his face in the darkness towards the steep, horribly tangled slope before him.

Brown knew nothing of the Galapagos Islands —truth to tell, he did not know that he was on one of them—and he was hardly expecting the appalling effort which the climb demanded. The island was only a mass of lava blocks welded together, overgrown with cactus; to make a yard's progress involved hauling oneself up a six-foot block guarded with razor edges, tearing through spiky cactus at the same time. In a very short time his hands and feet were raw, his clothes were in rags, blood was running from his scratches, and he was streaming with sweat in consequence of his violent exertion in that stifling atmosphere. After fifty yards of progress body and mind were numb with fatigue, but he still toiled on, the perfect fighting machine with duty as its motive power. One stray thought came through his dull mind and cheered him during that desperate struggle; that was that if his progress was so slow that of a landing party would be equally so, and with his rifle in a point of vantage he would be able to hold any number of men back. So, fumbling forward, gasping with fatigue, finding handhold and foothold in the dark, heaving himself up with gigantic efforts, occasionally lowering himself cautiously at breaks in the slope, he forced his way to the top, and there, on a projecting knuckle of rock which his instinct told him would be an advantageous strategic position, he lay down to wait until dawn, his rifle at his side. Instant sleep, the sleep of overstrain, closed over him as he lay, face downwards with his head on his arms.

CHAPTER XIII

BUT while Brown was crawling up the steep side of Resolution, and while he was asleep on the projecting saddle of rock, many things had happened. Tremendous news had reached *Ziethen* from the wireless stations on the American mainland; the whole ether of the Eastern Pacific had been in a chattering turmoil, for von Spee had struck his first blow upon the ring of enemies which had closed in upon him. Admiral Sir Christopher Cradock had encountered him, with two weak armoured cruisers against two powerful ones. He could have refused battle; he could have fallen back on a slow battleship which was wallowing along after him two hundred miles away, but he had refused to lose touch with an enemy who had already proved so elusive. He had gone boldly into action, hoping to do von Spee enough damage to cripple him, but he had not been so fortunate as had been *Charybdis* in her battle with *Ziethen*. *Good Hope* and *Monmouth* had sunk with all hands under the guns of *Scharnhorst* and *Gneisenau*, and von Spee was now for a brief space master of all the Southern Pacific coast. The nitrate ships, vital to the manufacture of British explosives, were cowering in Chile ports while von Spee, with all the prestige of victory, was lording it down the coast and an exasperated Admiralty in London was hurriedly searching for the wherewithal to close the gap which von Spee had hewn in the ring they had flung round him. In the last desperate matter of national life or death von Spee's victory was unimportant—what were two obsolete armoured cruisers to a Navy which could put thirty Dreadnoughts into line ?—but to the life of a Cabinet it was supremely important. With *Emden* still loose in the Indian Ocean sinking ships every day, with *Ziethen's* whereabouts unknown, so that at any moment a fresh series of depredations might clamour for public attention, and with von Spee triumphant in the Pacific, the Cabinet's prestige might well be so shaken as to ensure its fall; and the results of such an overturn were incalculable. Well was it, indeed, that *Ziethen* in her damaged condition had not dared to let loose her wireless and announce the destruction of *Charybdis*. Once let her repair herself so that she could move about and evade pursuit, and she would be emboldened to proclaim her victory; the streets of London would be full of posters: "Another Naval Disaster in the Pacific," and the Cabinet might come crashing down. That is what Captain von Lutz realized as he read the stream of wireless messages, and it was visualizations of this sort which fired him with impatience as he supervised the heeling of the ship and hastened below to inspect the achievements of the ship's smith and artificers who were preparing the plates which were to close the yawning hole in *Ziethen's* side. Not a moment was to be lost, although in all conscience Kapitan zur See von Lutz could see no cause for delay. Twelve hours from dawn would see those plates in position, *Ziethen* out once more in the Pacific, blazoning the destruction of *Charybdis* to all the world, and privately informing the German secret agent in Peru of her need for coal and of the rendezvous whither a collier should be sent.

Even the news that the captured English sailor had escaped and taken a rifle with him did not disturb Captain von Lutz's state of pleased anticipation; the escape of the sailor could do no harm—von Lutz wondered why the sailor had bothered to arm himself seeing that they would not trouble to pursue him—and the Captain contented himself with putting into prison the kindly sick-bay steward and the marine sentry of the upper deck, for purely disciplinary reasons.

Brown awoke when dawn was rushing into the sky. He was very sore and tired and thirsty; but he gratified his thirst only to the extent of two swallows from his water-bottle. He looked to his rifle. As he had hoped, the thick grease with which it had been smeared had kept the water from the metal, and no trace of rust appeared on it or in it. He opened the chamber of the butt, extracted oil-bottle and pull-through, and cleaned the barrel ready for action He had never before handled a Mauser rifle, but the supreme simplicity of the breech mechanism and sighting arrangements held no secrets for him. He filled the magazine and lay ready for action.

Below him, a scant quarter of a mile away, the *Ziethen* lay immobile nearly at the centre of the lagoon. The water round her was smooth, glassy, save for the strong ripple which Brown's powerful eyesight could detect about her stern and her anchor chains when the rapid tide swirled round them. She lay like a ship of the dead; even from her funnels there came only a shimmering hint of internal activity.

Yet as the light improved Brown could see white-clad figures on her deck and upper works, and he fingered his rifle, sighting on them each in turn, while refraining from pulling the trigger. He wanted every cartridge for more important work than casual killings. Later the white flag with the black cross soared upwards; the day was officially begun on board *Ziethen*. Immediately afterwards there was a stir of activity on the starboard side, and Brown's keen eyesight could see that the work he was expecting had begun. Two bo'sun's chairs were lowered down the side, one to each extremity of the hole made by *Charybdis'* shell, and a couple of white-clad figures scrambled down Jacob's ladders on to each of them. The damaged plates were to be unriveted and removed the while the new ones were preparing. Brown laid his rifle to his shoulder and his cheek to the butt.

During the brief while he was taking aim there was time for a myriad thoughts. If he did not press the trigger he would be left unpursued; *Ziethen* would effect her repairs and clear from Resolution, and he would remain, a free man, to take his chance of being picked up by a passing ship to serve his country again. Once let him fire and kill one of *Ziethen's* crew, and all the hundreds of German sailors on board would become his sworn enemies, and might hound him down to his death. Death lay on the one hand, and liberty on the other; it was a momentous choice and one over which Brown might have hesitated. He did not hesitate at all; he did not even think about the choice. He had made up his mind last night, and when a man like Brown makes up his mind there is no room left for hesitation.

Slowly the sights came into line. Through

the U of the backsight could be seen a tiny triangle of white—the white of the jumper of the man on the bo'sun's chair. Up into the U crept the wedge of the foresight; it moved steadily upward until its tip was exactly in line with the top of the U. There it stayed for a tiny instant of time, the while Brown, mindful of his musketry training at Harwich, and his periodical practises since, steadied his breathing, took the first pull off the trigger, and slowly squeezed the trigger back further through the final tenth of an inch. Then the rifle went off, and the echo of its report ran menacingly round the circle of the cliffs.

Maschinistmaat Zimmer had set cheerfully about his task of drilling out the rivets about the broken plate. He whistled to himself as he adjusted his tools, and he even cracked a joke or two with the three other men swinging beside him in the bo'sun's chairs. Tools and machinery had ever been a joy to him, and the prospect of using them, even after all this time, still cheered him up. He had no thought for his native Hamburg, nor even for the pretty, young blonde wife whom he had not seen for eighteen months.

He applied himself without a thought or a care to the work in hand. Then something hit him hard on the left side close to his heart, and for an instant of time he knew pain, agonizing pain, before darkness shut in upon him. He was dead as his knees gave way under him and he fell back over the rail of the chair ; his feet caught under the lower rail, and he hung head downwards, grotesquely inert. A bright splash on the plate where he had been working showed where the bullet which had passed through him had flattened. There was another widow now in Hamburg.

But no one at all paid any attention at that time to the dead body of Maschinistmaat Zimmer hanging by its knees, and certainly no one thought at all about his widow. Leading Seaman Brown saw him fall, snicked the bolt of the Mauser out and in, aimed again coolly and rapidly, and fired. The other man on Zimmer's bo'sun's chair fell dead even as he looked round to see what had happened to Zimmer ; one man on the other chair died as he turned to see whence came the firing ; the fourth man crumpled up as, panic-stricken, he sprang towards the Jacob's ladder to safety.

Brown fired three more shots into the groups of men who swarmed to the side of the ship on the upper deck out of curiosity; they took effect, and in a few seconds the upper deck was deserted as far as Brown could see. *Ziethen* swung idly at her anchors, grey and grim, with her big guns peering dumbly forth. At her side, absurdly small, the white corpse of Maschinist-maat Zimmer dangled head downward, and above him lay two white splotches which were the bodies of his mates. The fourth man had fallen into the sea.

It was an apt picture of the simultaneous power and helplessness of modern machinery. On the one hand lay *Ziethen*, with her ten 6-inch guns and her hundreds of crew and her horse-power reckoned in thousands, and on the other a lad of five foot eight, aged twenty, dominating her and enforcing his will upon her. But Brown was only powerful in consequence of his rifle, the handiest, neatest, most efficient piece of machinery ever devised by man. Not for the first time was the rifle altering the course of history. Brown was not a marvellously good shot, but to hit four men with four shots at a quarter of a mile when they are entirely exposed and conspicuous in white against a dark background does not call for marvellous shooting. Brown could handle his weapon in good workmanship fashion, and that is all the rifle demands. He had won the first trick, and he snuggled down into his niche on the saddle of rock to await the next development. A head appeared beyond *Ziethen's* foremost funnel, upon the bridge. He fired quickly, missed, and felt annoyed with himself.

On board the *Ziethen* there was annoyance at the tiresome incident; it would have remained mere annoyance save that five men had been killed. Were it not for the fury roused by the death of these men, messmates and friends, the attitude of *Ziethen's* officers and men would have been one of exasperated amusement—amusement that one man should dare to pit himself against an armoured cruiser, and exasperation at the delay to the repairing of the ship. From points of vantage—portholes, turret sighting slits—they scanned the cliffs anxiously to obtain a glimpse of this lunatic Englishman who was acting in so odd a manner.

Captain von Lutz, the angriest man on the ship, strode out upon the bridge; but a bullet smacked against a stanchion close at his ear and sang off into the distance. Even Captain von Lutz, one of the cleverest minds in the Imperial German Navy, marked out for high command in the near future, did not realize the difficulty of the task before him. He gave abrupt orders to clear away the steam pinnace, which had lain alongside since the night before, so that a landing party could arrest this irritating fellow and bring him on board to be dealt with.

Brown lay patiently in his niche. Where he lay he could command the stern and the whole starboard side of the ship. His rifle was pushed forward between two blocks of lava which gave him almost perfect protection; the straggling cactus was an efficient screen, and the bulge of the saddle and the nick in its tip gave him command of most of the face of the cliffs even where he lay. He was perfectly satisfied with his position; he saw that his magazine was filled and submitted patiently to the scorching heat, which was beginning to roast him slowly on his slab of naked rock.

Suddenly the next development made itself apparent. Round *Ziethen's* stern, shooting swiftly for the shore, came her steam pinnace, with twenty men aboard her. Brown's rifle cracked out again and again, taking swift toll before the men in her flung themselves down under shelter. The helmsman dropped, shot through the breast, but the officer in command, the gold flashing on his white coat, grasped the tiller and held her to her course as Brown's next bullet tore the cap from his head. Next second the boat was out of sight under the steep drop of the bare rock at the water's edge. Brown recharged his magazine.

The lieutenant in command of the landing party realized, in the instant that he grasped the helm, that this was not going to be the simple arrest of a nearly helpless man which he had anticipated. It dawned upon him that a man with a rifle a hundred yards away can take severe toll of a mass of men rushing upon him. There was a further lesson in addition to this which he was to learn, but that was yet to come. At present he made the arrangements which seemed satisfactory to him. He restrained the tendency of his men to bundle out of the pinnace and rush wildly up the slope. Under shelter of the steep bank he spread his men out over the fifty yards of the bank's extent. He saw that they had their rifles loaded. He got them all into position, and then he gave the word for a simultaneous rush.

But here began the second lesson. No one who had not attempted it could realize that the word "rush" had no place in the vocabulary of Resolution. The dreadful razor-edged blocks of lava and the clustered clinging cacti made anything like rapid progress impossible. An active man could move about on Resolution as fast as a snail in a garden, as Brown had discovered the night before.

Brown, motionless in his cranny, saw appear below him a line of men's heads at the water's edge, and he promptly put a bullet through one of them. The other heads developed shoulders and bodies and legs and came towards him, falling out of sight behind lava blocks, rising into full view again as they struggled over, creeping up towards him at an absurd, ridiculously slow pace. He fired slowly and deliberately, waiting for each shot until a man had heaved himself up into full view. A man's whole body at a hundred yards makes a superb target. Brown fired six shots and hit six men before the "rush" died away. No man seeing his companions killed at each side of him could bring himself to heave himself up and expose himself to the next shot. The dozen survivors stayed behind the cover they chanced to have at hand, and lay without attempting to make further upward progress. They pushed their rifles forward and began to fire up at the hidden death above them. The clatter and rattle of musketry began to resound round the island, shattering its stillness.

Yet, despite the numerical odds against him, all the advantages were still with Brown. No one yet in the attacking party had a clear knowledge of his hiding place; thanks to the two close blocks of lava and the cacti, he was thoroughly hidden. To an attacker all that might be in sight was a rifle muzzle and two or three square inches of face in deep shadow, and it would call for keener eyes, if unaided by chance, than the human race possessed to detect that much in the possible thousand square yards of rock and cactus where he might be hidden. Brown was not hampered to any such extent. He was higher up and could see farther over the edges of the lava blocks. He had more enemies to shoot at, and those enemies occupied positions taken up by chance in the heat of the moment. He was cool and unflurried by exertion. He knew the line his enemies had reached.

Bullets began to shriek overhead in the heated air, to raise clouds of pumice-dust when they hit the rocks, or to cut their way rustling through the fleshy cactus leaves. Not one came within ten yards of Brown. Coolly, cold-bloodedly even, he began to take toll of the attackers. Here there was a shoulder, there a leg, over there a head and shoulders completely exposed. He took deliberate aim and fired, shifted his aim, fired again, slewed round carefully to avoid any exposure of himself, and fired once more. Each shot echoed flatly round the cliff; in that heated air the noise of the report was no guide whatever to the position of the marksman. Shot after shot went home. Wounded men lay groaning in hollows and crevices. Dead men lay with their faces on their rifles. Very soon the few survivors dared not fire back, but crouched down in the advantageous bits of cover they chanced to be in, afraid to move lest this deadly enemy should send a bullet winging to their hearts. The firing died away. The lieutenant, mad with rage, leapt to his feet to shout to his men, and received a bullet full in the face which flung him over backward, a kicking, senseless huddle of limbs upon a cluster of spiny cactus. Then silence descended again. Brown blew gently down the breech of his rifle barrel, peered through fierce, narrowed eyes for any sign of his enemies, and resumed his patient, tense waiting, eyes and ears alert for any sign of activity down the cliff, where some rash enemy might be trying to creep unobserved up to him, or along the base of the cliff to outflank him. For an hour nothing happened save for one attempt on the part of an unfortunate to stretch his cramped limbs, an attempt which secured him a bullet through the knee which drained the life-blood out of him in half an hour.

So that a duel of patience ensued between the watcher on the cliff above and the dwindled half-dozen down below. After the rude reports of the rifles the eternal stillness of Resolution once more took possession. The sun climbed steadily upward, pouring down a stream of brassy heat upon the tortured rocks. The lagoon was of a vivid blue, and in the centre of it *Ziethen* swayed idly at anchor. As the heat increased the objects on the island took on a vaguely unreal appearance as the air above them shimmered hazily. Minutes dragged by like hours, but the crouching living sailors at the base of the cliff dared make no movement—not with the groans for help of their late wounded companion still remembered in their ears.

Over on *Ziethen* every one was puzzled at what had happened. They had watched the landing; they had seen men fall; they had heard the firing abruptly increase and die away to nothing; but they could not explain the sequence of events. They could still see the pinnace against the shore, and the boat guard sitting therein, but save for three or four dead bodies they could see nothing of the landing party, which was not surprising considering the tangle of rocks and cactus into which it had fallen. The opinion on board suddenly crystallized that the attack must have moved up into some gully unnoticeable from the ship, driving its quarry before it. At that rate the danger to workers on the damage must have vanished. Captain von Lutz, on fire with impatience to have his ship ready for action again, abruptly gave the order for a further party of artificers to recommence work.

Brown, up on his shelf of rock, saw the white-clothed figures, dwindled to the size of dolls, descend the Jacob's ladders. He gave them plenty of time; they sent up the bodies of their predecessors to the upper deck by a rope hoist, and then they began work. As they began he opened fire, and once again the echoes of his shots ran flatly round the island. The little white figures collapsed pitifully in the bo'sun's chairs. The sudden firing over their heads roused the men crouching down the cliff, and they, wearied with waiting and conscience-smitten about the non-fulfilment of their duty, took up their rifles once again. Some one down there had at last formed a shrewd guess as to where Brown was hidden, and as the rifles resumed their clatter bullet after bullet began to hit the rocks near him. One of them even drove dust into his eyes. Brown realized the danger. He paid no attention at present to the other riflemen firing at him, but, lying deadly still, peered this way and that through the slit between his two blocks of lava for this one keen-eyed or quick-witted enemy. He saw him at last—part of him, anyway. A bit of white jumper and dark collar, a hand and a cheek, deep in the shadow of a rock, and beyond the rock another bit of white which was probably the end of a trouser leg. Their owner was still firing away enthusiastically, and at each shot a bullet came buzzing nearby, or smacked against cactus and rock to go off at a new note. Remorselessly Brown took his aim, sighting for the edge of the collar against the white jumper. At a hundred yards he could not miss; as he pressed the trigger he saw the jumper jerk, and his target rolled struggling into view; some fair-haired boy, not so very unlike Brown himself, striving ridiculously to hold together his shattered right shoulder with his left hand, the blood pouring through his fingers and his face distorted with pain. Brown did not think twice about it. He turned his attention to the others, whose bullets were ploughing into the cliff face twenty yards on either side of him. One of them he killed, helplessly exposed to fire from above, and the fire of the others ceased abruptly again as they crouched down in their hollows. Even as they did so Brown observed that the boat guard, consumed with curiosity, was standing up trying to see what was going on, and in doing so exposing his head and shoulders over the rim of rock at the edge of the lagoon. Him Brown killed too, without mercy as without rancour.

It was nearly noon by now. Brown had delayed the repairs of *Ziethen* for six hours already. That in itself was a vast achievement.

CHAPTER XIV

THE next incident in the battle of Resolution was a tribute to Brown's power—to the power of the rifle which lay hot in his hand. There was a flutter of white from *Ziethen's* upper deck, a flutter of white long repeated. Then two figures climbed down the Jacob's ladders, and in one of them, even at that distance, Brown could recognize the rather portly form of the Surgeon who had condescended to crack a joke with him. Out of sheer rigidity of mental pose Brown found himself pointing his rifle at him before he remembered the white flag and desisted. The new-comers bent over the writhing figures on the bo'sun's chairs, busied themselves with bandages and splints, and soon (but every minute meant delay to *Ziethen*) the wounded men were hoisted inboard and their attendants climbed up after them.

And as they went there was a sudden commotion at the foot of the cliff. Some one there was too uncomfortable where he was. He could not bear the heat and the cramp and the strain any longer. Also he was the nearest to the water's edge—having had the steepest bit of cliff to ascend he had the easiest descent. He flung himself suddenly, on all fours, down a little precipice, rolled down another, crashed through a cluster of cactus on which he left bits of his clothes and of his skin, and tumbled over the last descent to the water. A bullet from Brown's rifle tore past his ear as he did so, but in his flustered panic he never noticed it

His example was infectious. The other survivors of the landing party rose simultaneously and flung themselves down the cliff. Brown smashed the spine of one of them as he gathered himself for his last leap, but the other two reached the water's edge—and safety—unhurt save for gashes and scratches. Three men now crouched in the steam pinnace; they were the only unwounded survivors of a landing party of twenty-one.

But to the puzzled, fuming officers on *Ziethen* their appearance by the pinnace meant relief from the worry of guessing what had happened to the landing party. The bridge semaphore began a series of staccato gesticulations, sending question after question to the dazed, conscience-stricken trio crouching in the lee of the rock edge. Sitting with their feet in the water (for if they stood their signalling hands came into Brown's view and within reach of his bullets) they produced a couple of handkerchiefs and signalled back—misspelt, badly signalled sentences went limping back to the cruiser, where dozens of pairs of keen eyes read off the halting words. Happily most of the questions asked could be answered in one word.

"Where is the rest of the party?"

"Dead."

"Where is Lieutenant Sturmer?"

"Dead."

"How many men opposed you?"

"One."

One question, however, the gesticulating semaphore demanded again and again, and the bothered sailors' blundering best constituted unsatisfactory replies.

"Where is the escaped prisoner?" demanded

the semaphore repeatedly, and the wretched men beside the pinnace struggled vainly to satisfy their persistent Captain.

"Up the cliff," they signalled, and "Hidden," and "We do not know," and "In the same place as he was this morning," and similar hopeless answers which drove Captain Lutz into a state of blind fury, which was not alleviated by the knowledge that part of the crew was reading off the answers and that the whole would know of them within the hour.

Exasperated officers raked the face of the cliff with powerful glasses, but there was no possible chance of their finding Brown in that way. The crew were furious with rage at the killing of the landing party. The last man shot by Brown in the bo'sun's chair had been smitten through both hips, and had lain shrieking with agony until the Surgeon reached him—and every shriek had been heard by the men. They were annoyed with their officers, and they thirsted, one and all, for the blood of the man who had put this shame upon their ship. And von Lutz knew all about it, as a good officer should. This insolent runaway had undone all the good effected by the victory over *Charybdis*, and only his death would restore good feeling. Von Lutz appreciated the need of good feeling in a crew about to set out on a voyage of half-senseless destruction with certain defeat sooner or later at the end of it. Besides, he must not allow the men to stay idle. Von Lutz had every possible motive when he issued orders to prepare for a landing at once of the largest party *Ziethen* could put on shore without entirely crippling herself—two hundred men. The news ran round the lower deck to the accompaniment of a buzz of joy.

Meanwhile the work of repair must go on. The Kapitan-Leutnant received his orders from the Captain. Some sort of screen for the workers must be arranged, so that the men at work on the injured plating could be hidden from the view of the rifleman on the cliff. A working party hurriedly fell upon the task of preparing booms and awnings—further delay for *Ziethen*.

Brown in his eyrie on the cliff might have found time heavy on his hands were he not so wholly absorbed in the possibility of the need for immediate action. The sun was slowly roasting him alive on the bare rock as though he were on a grid-iron. More than once he was forced to have recourse to one of his two water-bottles, and it was a worse torture to have to tear his lips away after a couple of grudging mouthfuls than it was to bear the thirst which preceded and followed them. Already one bottle was half empty, however, and Brown refused to allow himself anything approaching indulgence in the warm, metal-flavoured fluid. He sternly thrust back the cork and buckled the bottles to his belt. Small beauty is there in war—no one could find beauty in the tumbled bodies of the dead down below or in the tortured wounded calling feebly for water on the scorching rocks. But beauty could be found in that gesture of Brown's; one lone man—boy, rather—unwatched, unordered, putting aside the drink he craved at the call of what he considered his duty. He set his small white teeth while the sweat ran down his face and caked the streaked lava dust which grimed it, his rifle ever to his hand, suffering and enduring without regret or hesitation. The suffering and self-sacrifice and uncomplaining heroism which war has demanded, had they only been given to causes which mankind deems ignobler, could in the million years of man's existence have eliminated the need for suffering anywhere within mankind's sphere of activity. Brown, had this been pointed out to him, would not have thought such an end worth achieving at any price—most certainly not at the price demanded.

He took advantage of the lull to run the pull-through down his rifle barrel again. He looked with attention to the breech mechanism, for the lava dust was a serious clog to its smooth working. He counted his cartridges and settled them more handily in his pouches. He thought about having a meal, but put the idea aside; he was not at all hungry, and excitement and the sun pouring on to his back between them were not likely to allow him to be for some time. Still time dragged on.

Meanwhile, bent over the meagre charts of Resolution that were all any ship could boast, Captain von Lutz and his officers were planning the attack upon Brown which should put an end to the tiresome incident. This time nothing was to be left to chance. There was to be no repetition of the blunder of the morning, when too few men were flung idly upon an impossible climb in the face of a weapon of precision. The campaign was mapped out with real German thoroughness. All men were to carry food and water. Each landing party was allotted a different section of the island to beat through. As the small-arm supplies were limited, each party was carefully arranged in sections of beaters and riflemen. There was to be no taking of the bull by the horns. Brown's flanks were to be turned and he was to be forced upon the move first before he was directly attacked. The riflemen in the tops were to continue their watch for him—a bullet could travel from *Ziethen* to the island as easily as from the island to *Ziethen*. The hunt was to be continued all night if necessary. The capture or death of the quarry was to be broadcast by a prearranged whistle signal, whereupon the landing parties were to return immediately to the boats. All possible arrangements seemed to have been made; the only flaw was that the men who made the plans were still unaware of the difficulty of movement upon the island.

Brown, idling away the weary minutes, became aware of great activity on board *Ziethen*. The semaphore messages in German had of course been unreadable to him, and they had been the last incident of note, having occurred two hours ago. Now men began to show themselves here and there on the upper deck and boat deck. They exposed themselves no more than they could help, and Brown, firing rapidly when opportunity occurred, kept them harried. He hit at least four men, who dropped upon the upper deck, lying still or crawling away to shelter, and his shots were answered from the ship by hidden riflemen—who, all the same, had no knowledge of his exact position, and whose efforts in consequence caused him little trouble. A boom suddenly was run out on the starboard side abaft the bridge (Brown got in two shots into the little group he could see) and from it dropped a long strip of awning which quite screened the damaged area from his present position. At the same time another canvas screen was run up across the upper deck at the stern, and despite the elevation of his position he could not quite see over it. He sent three bullets through it, however, before he realized that this was a mere waste of priceless ammunition. The bridge semaphore wig-wagged again hysterically, and the result of its message was seen shortly, when the three wretched men in the steam pinnace left their shelter under the rock and made a wild dash back to the ship. The pinnace steered an erratic enough course, for the helmsman was lying flat on his back under the gunwale in his desperate anxiety to avoid fire, but all the same Brown could do her no harm and she soon shot round *Ziethen's* stern out of his sight into safety. The sound of bustle and activity even came across the lagoon to Brown's ears, but the screens hid everything from view save the ship's stern, upper works, and starboard side as far as the outboard screen, and he could not form any accurate dea of what was going on. He soon knew, however.

Out from *Ziethen's* port bow, where they had been manned out of his sight, shot four boats. The steam pinnace led, towing the other three, and they were all four crammed with men. A bubble of rifle-fire rose from *Ziethen* at the same time and now a new menace was added—machine guns. Two of these raved at him from *Ziethen's* fore-top, traversing slowly backward and forward across the suspected area, at each new traverse taking a line lower down the cliff. Bullets were sending the dust flying everywhere; the cactus was dropping here and there as the fleshy stems were cut through. Under that leaden hail Brown forced himself to think clearly. He could do little to stop those boats—the death of a dozen men would not stop them—and to fire he must expose himself a little in that deadly horizontal rain. It was not worth the risk. Brown crouched down into the hollow on the top of the saddle, behind the twin lava blocks which had served their turn so well. The sharp rap of a bullet upon one of them and the sound of others close above him made the propriety of the movement apparent immediately after. Then the hail passed on.

Brown, squirming round on his stomach, peered between the blocks, could see nothing, and squirmed round further to where he could see round them. The string of boats, instead of making straight for him, had dashed out through the opening of the lagoon, and even as he caught sight of them, had swung round to port, to his part of the island but on the outside, the sea face. His position was to be taken in reverse. It was then that Brown looked anxiously at the sun; there were still three hours more of daylight—only three hours, thank God.

The persistent beating of the machine-gun bullets started a little avalanche of rock thirty yards away on the right, and this disturbance attracted the attention of all the marksmen on the ship; bullets rained upon the spot until a wide dust cloud arose from it, drifting away on the hardly perceptible wind. Then the firing stopped; ammunition had been used in prodigious quantities, and even small-arm ammunition must not be allowed to run short on a raiding cruiser. From the ship came a rattle and buzz of machinery, and the creaking of tackle. Brown knew that the repairs were in progress, and he knew too that it would be hard for him to interfere for awhile; it made him frown in anguish. But while his face of the cliff was being raked by a dozen glasses, and while a score of marksmen, finger on trigger, were waiting anxiously for any sign of movement, he dared not make an open attempt to shift his position so as to be able to fire round the screen. Behind him, too, he knew that men were being landed at the outer margin of the island; soon they would be climbing up the outer face. Then they would reach the crest. His saddle of rock was dominated from one or two points on the crest. If the enemy reached one of those points in daylight he was certain ot death. It he moved from where he was by daylight he was certain of death. His life depended upon the coming of night. It may be at once taken for granted that Brown had no particular concern about the loss of his life; he was not yet oppressed by the fear of death. All he prayed for was the opportunity to continue to delay *Ziethen* at Resolution. He had done all he could do at present, all the same. With dogged determination he lay upon his ledge of rock waiting for night—or for the firing from the crest which would presage his death. There is a sublime, hard satisfaction in awaiting death when one has done all that could be done to avert it. Brown knew that satisfaction, even while he kept the cruiser under patient observation lest any further opportunity should display itself.

CHAPTER XV

THE steam pinnace, towing empty boats this time, suddenly shot into view through the break in the cliffs and dashed up to *Ziethen* ; in a quarter of an hour she shot out again with the boats full of men once more. Machine guns and rifles opened again from the ship upon the cliffs to prevent him from firing, but, as before, he had no intention of doing so. But he saw the boats turn to port as they had done the first time before the cliffs cut them from his view. That meant that the sweep across the island by a line of men, which Brown keenly foresaw, would only take place across a limited length ; if he could only move along the island sufficiently far he would evade the sweep. Two hundred men, which was Brown's accurate estimate of their number, at ten yard intervals cover two thousand yards, and the outside edge of Resolution is about four thousand yards in circumference. Brown realized that he must transfer himself to a point rather more than half-way round the island if he were to have any chance of escape.

Yet he could not move at all till nightfall. He waited on with anxious patience, not knowing from one minute's end to another when fire would be opened upon him from the crest of the island. Even Brown, with his sturdy, thoughtless resignation to Fate and Duty, cast anxious glances upward at the sun as it sank steadily in his face.

The seaward face of Resolution is very like the inner face, save that the angle of ascent is much less steep. The inner face is the nearly vertical wall of the throat of a crater; the outer face is the hardened remains of the lava flow. But on the outer face the blocks of lava resulting from sudden cooling are just as razor-edged and difficult of negotiation, and the cactus is just as impenetrable. The German landing party proceeded with German thoroughness. The first half was lined out along the seashore at accurate intervals, and was kept waiting until the second half was brought from the ship and lined out in continuation of it. Every man knew his job, which was to push straight up the face of the island ahead of him, keeping correct alignment and spacing, scanning every bush and cranny for the fugitive. The Lieutenant in command raced from one end of the line to the other in the steam pinnace, saw that everything was in order, and took up his position in the centre of the line. He gave the word and the line began its ascent.

Alas for accurate alignment! The weary climb up the seaward face was of necessity reduced in pace to that of the slowest, and the slowest was very slow. Not until it was really attempted could anyone guess the fiendish difficulty involved in moving about on Resolution. The frightful heat radiated from the rocks —which were nearly too hot for the naked hand —was the least of the difficulties. Cactus and lava combined to lacerate feet and hands. Two ankles were sprained in the first half-hour. The clumsy, rigid line made excruciatingly slow progress. Thirst descended instantly upon the sweating, swearing sailors, and the shirkers among them—there must always be shirkers in any large body of men—began to hang back and hold up their fellows. The fuming officers did their best by example and exhortation to keep the men on the move, but cramped living in a cruiser in the tropics is not the best preparation for a difficult piece of mountaineering. Here and there parts of the island were really unscalable, and men were compelled to move to one side to climb at all ; but as soon as the difficulty was evaded the petty officers, with the pedantic adherence to orders resulting from an over-strict discipline, held up their sections of the line until the intervals were corrected. No one could see very far to the left or right, thanks to convexity of the face and the lunatic roughness of the surface, so that any attempt to command or lead the whole line on the part of the Lieutenant was quite hopeless. Bound by its first rigid orders, the line crawled up the face of the island at a pace much slower than even the slowest among them could have proceeded alone.

An hour before nightfall (at least an hour, that is to say, later than he had expected to reach the crest) the exasperated Lieutenant sent word along the line for each man to push on as best he could. But it takes time to pass orders from mouth to mouth along an extended line, and only one-third of the distance had been covered when they were issued. The sun sank gaudily into the purple sea and night fell with dramatic rapidity to find Brown still unfired at, and two hundred German sailors spread out and tangled in the darkness over a mile of leg-breaking rock.

Brown waited with sturdy, unyielding patience for complete darkness. Throughout the afternoon he had been peering down the cliff below him, mapping out in his mind a path down the cliff—a handhold here, a foothold there, a slide lower down. When night came he was ready; his hands were bound about with strips torn from his jumper, his equipment fastened about him, his mind as resolute as ever. He was glad that the German landing party had not caught him, but it was a temperate gladness, in no way to be associated with thankfulness. It did not occur to him to be thankful. Without a regret or a thought save for the business in hand, he climbed off the shelf which had been his fortress for twelve hours and swung himself down. The cruel lava tore and hacked at him as he slid and tumbled down the cliff. The razor edges tore through his shoes and cut deep into his feet. The cactus spines scratched great cuts into his body, making long lines like the marks of a tiger's claws. He wrenched ankle and knee so that they pained him excruciatingly. Yet he kept in his mind the various points to be aimed at, and it was not long before he had covered the three hundred feet of descent and had reached the place of his landing the day before.

The first, ill-fated German landing party had reached the island a hundred yards away to his right, and it was there that the tumbled, tossed bodies of its dead lay along with the dozen wounded whose pitiful cries had climbed the rock to Brown's ears all the afternoon. Gladly would Brown have gone to them, have tried to tend their hurts and given them the water for which they had moaned unceasingly, were it not that to do so would have imperilled the execution of his duty. As it was, he shut his ears to the pitiful sounds, just as he had done all day, and proceeded with his task. Nothing could weigh in the scale at all against his conception of what he had to do. Several of the wounded died that night.

His two lifebelts still lay in their cactus clump, and he picked them out and buckled them round himself and his rifle as on the preceding night. Then he lowered himself into the water and set out across the lagoon. The sea-water added intensely to the pain of his cuts and scratches.

The Germans had acted in disagreement with one of Napoleon's best-known maxims of war—one should only manœuvre about a fixed point; to have done so he needed to be held, pinned to his position by a menace from the front. With the coming of darkness he was free to move about as much as physical conditions would allow, and that, as long as the lagoon was open to him, was a considerable amount. All the German turning movements, all their advances upon his rear and his flanks, were useless. Their blows were blows in the air as long as Brown could evade them.

Brown paddled steadily round the lagoon fifty yards from shore, keeping away from the ship. Far behind him, on the unseen face of the island, the wretched German sailors were labouring and toiling as they pursued their stumbling way over the lava. Cut feet and sprained ankles and broken wrists occurred regularly. The island was alive with the clash and clatter of dropped rifles and stumbling feet. No one knows who fired the first shot. Most probably it was an accident, the result of a stumble by some fool (there are always fools to be found among two hundred men) who had slipped a cartridge into his rifle. The noise of the shot echoed through the darkness. Brown, paddling across the lagoon, heard it and wondered. The example was infectious. Bewildered men all along the straggling line began to load their rifles, and it was only a matter of seconds before the rifles went off. The scared iguanas, nocturnal creatures, scurrying over rocks and round bushes, gave frights to various people, and there was quite a respectable bubble of musketry round the island before the whistles of the officers and the shouted orders brought about a cessation of fire. The fact that no one was hit by the hundreds of bullets which went whistling in all directions is simply astonishing. On board *Ziethen* the sound was accepted as a welcome proof that the murderous fugitive had met his fate, the while Brown steadily made his way across the lagoon to a point on the shore broad on *Ziethen's* starboard beam. Here, with some difficulty, he found a place where he could land, and once more he let drop his lifebelts into a cluster of cactus. Then he set his teeth and began to try to climb the steep cliff.

But his cuts and his bruises and his stiffness and the awful rawness of his feet reduced his activity to a pitifully small minimum. Climb he must if he were to maintain for another day his annoyance of *Ziethen*. He must be high enough to be able to beat off attacks from the shore and to dominate *Ziethen's* deck. Also he must be close in to the foot of an overhanging bit of cliff if he was to have any security against fire from above, and it would be as well if he had cover to his left and right in addition, seeing that there were scores of riflemen at large upon the island seeking his death. What he needed was something like a cave half-way up the cliff, and for this, in the light of the late-rising moon, he peered about anxiously between his convulsive, agonized efforts to scale the successive precipices of the cliff.

His rifle and ammunition too were serious hindrances to his progress, and the sweat poured off him and his face was distorted with strain at each heartbreaking struggle. Both his feet and his hands left bloody imprints upon the rock where they touched it. Yet he struggled on, upwards and sideways, to where in the faint light he thought he could make out a shallow vertical cleft in the cliff face which might be suitable for his purpose. It was long past midnight before he reached it, passed judgment upon it, and roused himself to one further struggle, despite the stubborn reluctance of nerves and sinews, to climb yet a little higher to a better place still. There he fell half fainting upon the harsh lava.

Even then, after half an hour's rest, he fought his way back to consciousness again and raised his head and eyed *Ziethen*, whose malignant bulk, black in the faint light, swam on the magical water of the lagoon. On her starboard side, square to his front, hung a faint patch of light, and the noise of riveters came to his ears over the water. The hole in the ship's side, screened forward and aft, and partly screened in front, had been lit up by electric lights dangled over the side, and there the repairing crews were toiling to replace the damaged plates and striving to make up for the six hours' delay Brown had imposed upon them. Through the gaps in the outer screen Brown could just see on occasions human figures moving back and forth, and with a snarl of fainting determination he slid his rifle forward. But he checked himself even as his finger reached the trigger. He was too shaky after his exertions to be sure of hitting hard and often without too many misses. Besides, a rifleman, however invisible by daylight, shows up all too plainly by night by reason of the flash of his weapon. With enemies possibly within close range he dared not (for the love of his duty, not of his life) expose himself to this danger without adequate chance of return. Brown's fighting brain weighed all these considerations even while every fibre of his body shrieked with agony, and he reached a sound conclusion. He laid his rifle down, and then, before even he could settle himself comfortably, he collapsed on to the rifle butt. No one knows whether he fainted or slept, or both. And meanwhile the two hundred men of the landing party stumbled and blundered and swore as they endeavoured to sweep across the island, and still fired a stray shot or two when the strain became too much for their nerves.

CHAPTER XVI

BROWN woke, or regained consciousness, just as dawn was climbing brilliantly up the sky. His first action was to drink temperately from the dwindling supply in his second water-bottle. His cracked lips and lava-impregnated mouth and throat permitted of no choice of action. Then, doggedly, he began to make sure of his position and situation. Looking out of his notch in the cliff face, hoisting himself cautiously on his knees to do so, he saw a dozen white figures creeping slowly on the very crest of the island a quarter of a mile from him. On the inner face of the island, round about his previous position, he saw about a dozen others perched precariously here and there, still endeavouring to carry out their fantastic orders to sweep the island from one sea to another. Of the rest of the landing party Brown could see nothing, but he could guess shrewdly enough.

They were scattered hither and thither over the outer face of Resolution, perhaps still struggling on, perhaps nursing cut feet or broken ankles, perhaps sleeping or dodging duty in the way unsupervised men will. Brown shrank down into his notch again ; he was safe enough from observation, and out of sight, indeed, of nearly every point of the island.

In front, however, *Ziethen* was in full view. The gay screens hung out over the damaged part were like a box applied to the ship's side—a box defective down one edge, however. Through the gap Brown could see occasionally a white figure appear and disappear, although for the moment the noise of the hammers had ceased. Actually, with the removal of the damaged plates, the operation now in progress was the lowering down of the new plates to be riveted into position. It was in consequence of the demands of the tackle for this business that the booms of the screens had been shifted to leave the small gap Brown noted ; and as Brown had not fired at the ship for fifteen hours a certain carelessness had been engendered, to say nothing of the fact that *Ziethen* believed, and could hardly help believing, that the landing party had killed Brown hours ago.

Brown pulled the oily rag through his rifle barrel ; he oiled the breech, which was beginning to stick badly, and then he sighted carefully for the gap in the screen. He awaited the most favourable moment and then fired twice, quickly, and he killed the two men he could see. Then, to make the most of his surprise, he fired again and again through the screen, scattering his shots here and there across it and up and down it. He actually, although he did not know it, hit one or two men, and his misses were quite efficacious also, in that they scared into jumpiness the men they did not hit. The moment when a ten-ton steel plate is swinging in tackles is a bad moment to be shot at.

The killings and the wounds and the interruption roused *Ziethen* to a pitch of fury previously unreached. Those on board were maddened by the deaths of their friends, and they were furiously angry with the landing party, who had so absurdly failed in its mission. Captain von Lutz, in a flaming rage, set the bridge semaphore into staccato action, and the wretched Lieutenant in command on shore, staggering bleared-eyed along the crest after a sleepless night of fevered action, read the messages he sent with a sick feeling at his heart. The vivid sentences poured out by the gesticulating semaphore as Captain von Lutz vehemently demanded what on earth the Lieutenant and landing party were about stung the wretched officer to the quick. A Japanese lieutenant would have committed suicide; a German one merely called out his last reserves of energy and tried to gather a body of the less faint-hearted and push on round the island to where Brown lay hidden.

On board *Ziethen* work was suspended temporarily—another triumph to Brown's credit. Too many skilled ratings had been lost already for the Captain to order his remaining ones to take the chance of the bullets which Brown was sending at intervals through the screen. Instead he decided to turn *Ziethen* away from the point of attack, and to turn an unwieldy armoured cruiser, with her five hundred feet of length, and listing badly at that, in a lagoon wherein the tide was swirling in a whirlpool, was an operation calling for care and consuming much time. The two anchors had to be raised, the propellers set in motion, and *Ziethen* gently nursed into position, one anchor dropped, the set of the current combated, and then the other anchor dropped—and good holding ground was scarce in that fathomless crater. Altogether it was an hour before the delicate operation of mooring was completed and the delicate operation of lowering the new plates into position was resumed. Brown heard at length the clatter of the riveting, and knew that the delays he had imposed upon *Ziethen* were ending at last.

But the labours of the landing party were still in full blast. The Lieutenant found it hard to move any sort of force along the island. His two hundred men were scattered over a mile of almost impossible country, and the problem of supplies suddenly leaped into prominence and added another burden to the Lieutenant's overloaded shoulders. Every man had landed with a day's water; they had been violently exerting themselves for nearly twenty-four hours, and nine men out of ten had consumed the last drop of their water several hours back. The Equatorial sun, mounting steadily higher, called the attention of every one to his overwhelming thirst. The unhappy Lieutenant signalled to his captain that he could not hope to move without water. Captain von Lutz signalled back in blistering fashion, but the Lieutenant, under the spur of most dire and urgent necessity, held to his contention. The Captain, raging, sent off water to him round the island, and his Commander as well, to take over control, under strict orders not to return without bringing back Brown, dead or alive.

For the moral situation was serious. No captain could dream now of setting out on a long and arduous cruise with a crew in such a temper as *Ziethen's* was. Thirty-four men killed and wounded (their loss alone would be a serious nuisance with prize crews to be thought of) and two ignominious reverses had upset discipline to a tiresome extent. If *Ziethen* were to sail away without taking vengeance on Brown the crew would lose all respect for their officers. And discipline would be under severe strain on a raiding voyage, with its necessary accompaniments of coaling at sea, and loot, and imminent prospects of a fight. Captain von

Lutz, weighing all factors in the situation, decided that Brown must die, even though killing him meant prolonging their dangerous sojourn in the vicinity of land and postponing their ravening onslaught upon British shipping.

So the water was sent, and the Kapitan-Leutnant took over the command; and he did not find it an easy burden. To distribute water among his scattered, weary command, each individual of whom was stuck where he was nearly as effectively as a fly upon a fly-paper, consumed hours of time and much of the strength of the twenty men he brought as reinforcements. It was afternoon before he was ready to make his first move, and by that time the riveting on *Ziethen* was completed and she was a whole ship again, ready to steam out of Resolution. Brown could now credit himself with further delays to her—all the length of time, in fact, which he occupied in dying.

The Commander acted with energy. He sent his casualties—heat-stroke, broken ankles, cut feet—down the cliff to where the first landing had been made. There the men Brown had wounded the day before at last received attention and water; the dead and wounded were sent back to the ship for attention or burial, but all this was in rear of the Commander's head-quarters and main line of assault. Having purged his force of its weaker elements, the Commander proceeded to make his way along the crest of the island, while a boat with full crew lay ready to dash to any point to which it might be signalled, and another one landed more men across the opening of the lagoon to cut off any attempt Brown might make to evade attack again. The Commander, thrusting aside with contempt the expostulations of the Lieutenant he had superseded, still did not realize the hopelessness of movement on the land, or, if he did, he did not care how much time the business consumed as long as it was done thoroughly. From *Ziethen's* bridge he had watched the failure of the first frontal assault, and he was not going to throw away another dozen lives in that fashion. These long, weary flanking movements were the alternative, and he accepted it stoically. All the same, a day of little water and a night of no rest had taken most of the heart out of his men, and it was woefully slow progress that he made. Night came down and found his men still tangled utterly in the crevasses of Resolution. It found Brown too lodged in his cleft in the cliff, tormented with thirst, running a dry tongue round his cracked lips, agonized by the pain in his hands and feet, bitten in every part of his body by the vicious flies, but all the same without a thought of surrender. That simply did not occur to him. It was not consonant with his heredity nor with his childish training.

CHAPTER XVII

HERR HANS SCHMIDT lay sleeping peacefully and noisily in his porch in Panama. He lay on his back; when he went to sleep his hands had been crossed upon his stomach, but with the passage of time they had slid down the incline until now they lay on his chest, so that his attitude was entirely one of peace and resignation. Beside him Frau Schmidt slumbered just as peacefully and not quite as noisily; for the Schmidts believed in maintaining the good old tradition of the family double bed despite the heat of the tropics.

Verily was Herr Schmidt entitled to the blissful sleep which comes of a sense of completed duty. He was head of the German unofficial representatives on the Pacific coast, and all his work so far had been thorough and successful. He had gleaned from stray references the strength of Admiral Cradock's squadron and he had reported it to Admiral von Spee, and the result had been obvious at Coronel. At Guayaquil and Callao he had colliers ready to sail on the instant—one of them, thanks to lavish expenditure of funds and jugglery with papers, actually under the British flag. Should von Spee decide to return northwards from Coronel he would find abundance of best Welsh steam coal awaiting him, or if *Ziethen* turned up unexpectedly there would be the same kindly reception ready for her. Everywhere German agents were seeking bits of news to report to him, so that he could piece them together and pass them on. He knew all about the British battle cruiser in the West Indies, and he could name the ships which were watching lest German commerce destroyers should push out of American Atlantic ports; he did not know, all the same, about Admiral Sturdee's fleet which was fitting out in England, but for that he bears no blame. The discovery of the object of this squadron was the business of the central organization, which failed lamentably. No, Schmidt had done everything that could be expected of him, and he was fully entitled to the blissful sleep which encompassed him and which was about to be so rudely interrupted.

The telephone at the bedside rang sharply, and Schmidt started up, blinking himself into rapid wakefulness. Beside him his wife muttered heavily, humped over on her side, and clawed her tangled hair out of her eyes. She switched on the light while Schmidt pulled back the mosquito net and reached for the telephone instrument.

The first sounds to reach his ear were apparently meaningless gibberish, but it seemingly did not disconcert him. He uttered gibberish in reply, and with password and countersign thus exchanged his agent could safely pour forth his news into Herr Schmidt's receptive ear. The torrent of rapid German was of an import which made Herr Schmidt start in surprise.

"What?" he demanded. "Where are they now?"

"They were going through Gatun when I tried to telephone first, sir," came the answer. "They must be almost at the Cut now."

"But why did I not hear of this at once?" demanded Herr Schmidt savagely.

The voice at the receiver fell away into a placatory whine.

"I couldn't, sir. Really, sir. Those two Englishmen here were too closely after us. They've taken Schulz. I'm sure they have. I've told you about them often before. I simply couldn't get a line to Panama before this. They were all too busy, sir."

"Rubbish!" exploded Herr Schmidt. "You Gatun set are a gang of cowards and worse. You say you don't even know the battle cruiser's name?"

"No, sir. Couldn't get it anyway. But it's a battle cruiser for certain. Twenty thousand tons. And the light cruiser's the *Penzance*."

"Bah!" said Schmidt. "Get her name at once. And all about her—where she comes from and what she's doing. If you can't do that in Gatun you're not on my pay list any more. Report again in two hours' time."

Schmidt slammed down the receiver and heaved himself out of bed. His hairy legs protruded beneath his brief nightshirt, and there was a hint of hairy chest at its open throat. He put on his thick round glasses with one hand and reached for his trousers with the other. While pulling on his trousers he thrust his bare feet anyhow into his shoes. Then, with a growl at his wife, he went clattering out of the house to the garage. Three minutes later, in the growing light of dawn, his car was roaring out of Panama with its headlights blazing, while Schmidt, thick body bent, grasped the wheel in his big hairy hands. Out of Panama he went, with his car leaping madly over the fantastic bumps and hollows of the country road. He tore through the ruins of Old Panama and onward where the road degenerated into a mere track at the spot where the Canal Zone adjoined the Republic of Panama. A steady hand and powerful wrists were necessary to hold the car to the track, but burly Hans Schmidt was a brilliant driver. He swung aside on to an even narrower path where the undergrowth crashed beneath his wheels and tore at the body. Uphill he went, his foot steady on the accelerator, until the path ran into a small clearing beyond which stood a tall half-ruined building which, nevertheless, by its patching and by the condition of its courtyard, showed signs of recent occupation. Here Schmidt stopped the car, and with an agility unexpected in one of his bulk he scrambled out and rushed into the building and up the rotten stone stairs.

The tall room at the top of the tower was modern in its furnishings ; indeed, the modernity was carried to an extreme pitch, for the main part of the furniture comprised a receiving and transmitting wireless plant of the highest possible power. The old ruined tower, once a fortress which had been taken and sacked by Morgan and his buccaneers two-and-a-half centuries ago, was now one of the central ganglia of the German Pacific secret service. On a camp bed at one side of the room lay a young man, half asleep ; at the table by the instruments sat another, with the receivers on his ears. They both looked up when Herr Schmidt entered, but they were treated with scant courtesy. Schmidt's first action was to jerk head and thumb back to the door, and they rose slowly to obey. The one with the instruments offered Schmidt the bearing pad the messages recently intercepted—all sorts of messages, in code and *en clair*, mercantile and military—but Schmidt cast it aside after flipping through its pages and running an eye over the messages.

"Outside," he growled, "quickly."

They went, shambling, while Schmidt threw himself into the chair, adjusted the receiver, and began tuning in the instruments with his thick hands, making the adjustments for a general call with steady delicacy. From a pocket at the back of his trousers he produced a small book printed on fine paper; and with a stub of pencil and a scrap of writing paper he made a note or two, constantly referring to the book. Soon the message he had in mind was written in code on the paper; with his heavy face upturned to the ceiling he memorized it, and then, striking a match, he burnt the piece of paper bearing his notes. The code book was thrust back into his pocket, and above it, inside the pocket, he adjusted the fish-hook which was fastened in the lining. The unwary hand which dived into that pocket in search of Germany's most secret naval code would be lacerated and torn excruciatingly. Then Schmidt set about broadcasting his message, sending it out again and again. His sub-stations at Callao and Valparaiso would take it in and relay it; the cables would bear it by devious routes back to Germany. Von Spee on the Chilean coast would receive it; the *Ziethen*, lost somewhere in the Pacific, would take it in as well. Hour after hour Schmidt sent out that message, sitting in his grotesque garb of nightshirt and trousers while the sweat ran down his unshaved cheeks and heavy jowl. It was not the sort of message he could trust to subordinates.

For the tremendous naval strength of England was to be exerted against von Spee's squadron. There was to be no more attempts to engage him with armoured cruisers or obsolete battle-ships. There was a new power at the Admiralty—Fisher, who had become First Sea Lord at the time of the disaster at Coronel. Von Spee was to be hounded down and exterminated. Battle cruisers were to be used, the most deadly enemies of the armoured cruiser. Admiral Sturdee was to be sent from England with *Invincible* and *Inflexible* and half a dozen modern cruisers round the Horn to sweep northwards up the

Pacific. But this part of the plan was unknown to Schmidt—it was unknown to any German until von Spee at the Falklands saw the tripod masts of the battle cruisers and read his death in that sight. The southward sweep was what concerned Schmidt at the moment.

H.M. battle cruiser *Leopard* had been stationed for three weeks already in the West Indies; there she could guard against von Spee, or any detachment from his force, passing the Panama Canal and ravaging the rich English shipping of the Caribbean and the Gulf, and there also she could be ready to cut off any movement of the Germans northward round the Horn. But to the new personality at the Admiralty any such defensive attitude was distasteful and obnoxious. *Leopard* must be used offensively. Let her pass the Canal herself, instead of waiting for the Germans to do it; let her seek out the enemy instead of waiting passively for the enemy to come within her grasp. It was the truer, more decisive strategy, and the orders were passed to *Leopard* on the same day that the other orders were given to Admiral Sturdee.

So that *Leopard* and her attendant light cruiser

Penzance had passed out of the West Indies and the cognizance of the German agents there, and was even now making the passage of the Canal, the first ship of all Britain's fleet to make use of the waterway—one month open, only. The whining voice on Herr Schmidt's telephone had told him of her passing Gatun lock, and now, while Schmidt was broadcasting his warning to all who might read it, she was going through Miraflores lock and her bow was wet with the salt water of the Pacific. Her twenty-four knots and her 12-inch guns meant death to any German ship on that ocean; small wonder, then, that Herr Schmidt received the news so gravely, and small wonder that he prayed to his German God that the electrical disturbances of the Pacific would not prevent the reception of the warning he was sending out. With the damp, sticky heat calling forth the sweat from every pore he bent again and again to his duty, his masterful hands tapping out the staccato Morse at regular half-hour intervals. He did his duty thoroughly, as every German did. From down below came the faint thud-thud of the engine and the deep hum of the dynamo;

the shrill whine of the mosquitoes circling round his sweating head blended with the hum. They bit the back of his thick neck, and they sought out his uncovered ankles.

CHAPTER XVIII

ALBERT BROWN had spent a weary night. Before morning he had used the last of his water, and his thirst occupied nearly all his thoughts. His hunger had led him to eat some of his tinned provisions, and that, of course, increased his thirst inordinately. From the cessation of the noise of the riveting on board *Ziethen* he deduced that repairs were completed, but as long as a landing party was on shore it was his duty to go on fighting and keep it occupied, and so detain *Ziethen* longer still at Resolution. He fought down his thirst, and he fell now and again into a troubled sleep, from which he awoke each time with a start and listened to the clamorous noises made in the otherwise still night by the landing party.

It is difficult to imagine the condition of the surface of Resolution. Think of a stretch of mud exposed to the sun. It cracks in all directions, breaking up into small cakes. The lava of Resolution has done the same thing; the pieces of lava of which it is composed are of much the same size and shape as a dining-room table would be if it were solid down to the ends of its legs, and the cracks between the pieces vary in depth from one to ten feet. Now realize that the edges of each cake are sharp as knives, and that the surfaces of each cake are seamed with minor cracks whose edges are equally sharp. Add to this the facts that landslides and earthquake action have tumbled the blocks over each other higgledy-piggledy, and that the general slope of the whole mass is on one side steeper than the roof of a house and on the other nearly as steep. Finally, dot the whole slopes with intensely spiny cactus, and a faint mental picture can be formed of the difficulty of progress over them in the dark, especially when hampered by thirst on a hot night. A hundred yards in an hour is a high speed—six hundred yards in six hours is impossible.

This was the lesson which each officer of *Ziethen* had to learn in turn, and which each refused to accept as truth from his junior. The Commander doubted what the Lieutenant said about it, and Captain von Lutz, who, of course, did not leave his ship, doubted both the Commander and the Lieutenant. When morning came and found Brown still alive and untaken (he informed every one of the fact by sending a couple of bullets along *Ziethen's* bridge, narrowly missing the officer of the watch), pleasant expectation on board changed to furious consternation.

The semaphore came into action to goad the unhappy Commander with a proper sense of his failure. Captain von Lutz interfered with the plans of the Commander, and abruptly sent the last fifty men who could be spared from the work of the ship in a dash for the inner shore in an assault upon the place where he judged Brown to be. He was only one hundred yards out in his estimate of the line; that was good judgment, not bad, considering that he had only the noise of rifle shots echoing from a cliff to guide him, and that *Ziethen*, thanks to her turn away, was now nearly half a mile from Brown.

Brown saw the boats coming and turned his rifle upon them, but now, with his teeth chattering with fever and his hands trembling, he could not make even moderately good practice. He knew that Fate was close upon him as he looked along the rifle barrel and saw the foresight dancing like a live thing in the U of the backsight, and as shot after shot went wide. But the rifle is a sweet tool, and gives of its best even in bungling hands as far as in it lies. Twice Brown loosed off, almost by accident, at the right moment, and each time a man in one of the boats collapsed upon his thwart. Two casualties could not stop the boats. They rushed in to the foot of the cliff and the boats' crews bundled out, just as in the first misguided attempt, scattering a little swarm of *Amblyrhincus*—marine iguanas—who had been comfortably feeding on seaweed at the water's edge regardless of the din of battle echoing round the island.

Even at a hundred yards Brown found that he made but poor practice. He dropped two men only in five shots, and then, reaching into his pouches to refill his magazine, he realized that only two of them were full; he had only twenty rounds left. With such a small reserve he knew that he could hardly stop this close attack—and the one which must develop soon out on his left would be able to push forward unopposed. It was the last, desperate death grapple. Brown's lips parted in a harsh grin so that the black cracks upon them showed in deep contrast with his white teeth. He pulled his failing strength together for one more effort, steadied his weak limbs, and tried to shoot the attackers down deliberately, one by one.

More than one of the struggling attacking party dropped, but far more by reason of the difficulties of the ascent than in consequence of the casualities the forward impetus died away. Just as before the climbers crouched down in hollows and crannies; from the sound of Brown's firing they had formed some idea of his position, and they began to fire back at him. Once more Brown heard the sharp noise of bullets passing close beside him, and once more little puffs of lava dust arose here and there where the bullets struck. But on this occasion the attack had begun farther off to one side and Brown was not perched quite so high up. So that his position was not nearly so dominating, and he could not overlook the lumps of rock behind which lay his enemies. Only here and there could he see small portions of the bodies of the men firing at him, and in his shaking condition he could not hit these with certainty or anything approaching certainty. He caused another two casualties, but these did not deter the forty men who were firing at him, and when he had filled his magazine with his last cartridges he had to keep these in reserve to use against the last rush. He lay as close to the lava as he could, awaiting in uncomplaining patience for the end to come, while the bullets crackled and sang all round about him.

Soon his quiescence was noted by those below; the bolder and the stronger among them heaved themselves up and made little advances up the face of the cliff from one block to another, out of one crevice into the next. Before long most of the line was bellying forward, up the cliff, and working along it, emboldened by the cessation of Brown's fire. Only half a dozen men, the less energetic or the fainter hearted, still lay crouched in their cover and maintained a hectic fire on the patch where they thought Brown lay. They wasted ammunition at an amazing rate, but they made an encouraging noise even if they did nothing else. Brown, peering with one eye over the edge, could see two or three men actually only twenty yards below him and fifty yards away. Soon one of them would get a clear sight of him, and that would be the end. He felt no resentment, either against Fate or against the men who were about to take his life; he had done all he could.

And at that very moment the battle was interrupted. A tremendous braying from *Ziethen's* siren called every one's attention clamorously to the signal which was being wig-wagged rapidly and repeatedly from her bridge semaphore. It was the general recall.

For some minutes the attackers hesitated. It was hard to go back when success was so close at hand. But the siren brayed again, and the semaphore gesticulated feverishly. No one could act in independence of orders so definite and so oft repeated. Reluctantly the officer commanding the laning party blew his whistle and the attackers turned back down the cliff, crawling back perilously, dropping down little precipices, more slowly than they would have gone had their effort been successful. Brown saw them go, and as a last effort he raised himself and sent a bullet through the shoulder of the officer in command—which had the very desirable effect of delaying the retreat while the landing party turned and wasted much further ammunition upon him until the further trumpetings of *Ziethen's* siren recalled them to duty. They dropped down to the boats, lifted in their wounded and dead, and pulled slowly back to the cruiser.

Nevertheless it was not the evacuation of the island by the landing party which took up so much time ; the real delay was caused by the huge, useless, straggling mob on the outer face. After the Commander in charge had read the signals from the vantage point on the crest he had so painfully gained he had still to pass the word for retreat throughout the length and breadth of his straggling command, and having done so he still had to get his men down to the beaches. Most of them had been straying loose over Resolution for nearly forty-eight hours; they were dispirited, lame, fatigued, and most woefully undisciplined. Many of the lazy and insubordinate among them had found crannies here and there and were stretched out fast asleep in some tiny area of shade. In the blinding noonday heat even the best of the men moved slowly when the heart was taken out of them by the order to retreat, and many of them strayed back in directions quite opposite to the one the Commander desired. The frightful heat of the rocks, enough to blister a bare hand laid upon them, discouraged activity; men who would struggle cheerfully forward into action would soon cease to struggle when defeat, and that by a single man, had to be admitted. The Commander and the Lieutenant raved and swore as much as their dry throats permitted, while the sweat drenched their soiled ducks; the petty officers struggled to keep the men within earshot of them on the move; but it was a painful, hopeless task. A man a hundred yards away might as well be ten miles away for all the use it was giving orders to him—there was no going back to him without wasting another hour.

To the wretched Commander on the crest the hours after noon seemed to race by; the sun seemed to sink towards the horizon at three times its usual speed, while the messages spilt out by the accursed semaphore became more and more caustic. He watched the incredibly slow progress of his men down to the boats with fever consuming his soul. There seemed no end to the white-clad figures who came into sight one after the other, round the bulge of the island at ten minute intervals—and some of them were actually still trying to make their way up to the crest instead of down to the boats.

Seaman Muller, the ship's bad character, came struggling along the top of the crest past the Commander. His feet were very sore and his clothes were in tatters, and his gait was, to use a homely simile, like that of a cat on hot bricks. With his rifle hitched over his shoulder he was picking his way along the more easy stretch of small lava at the top of the island.

He came within fifty yards of the blaspheming Commander, who shouted to him to get away diagonally down the slope to the boats, but Seaman Muller made an inaudible reply—he was not a very disciplined character at the very best of times. He was certainly not going to plunge down into that awful inferno of rocks and cactus until he had to. He would keep along the crest until he was above the boats, and then he would, perhaps, graciously go down the steep slope. Until then he was going to keep to this easier part of the island—easier, but most uneasy. He hitched his equipment about him and continued the agonizing effort of struggling up and down the lava blocks.

A hundred yards past the Commander he stopped to rest. He sat down where a lava block now cast a fair amount of shade, thanks to the setting of the sun. He mopped his streaming face; he considered his thirst and went off into a happy dream, imagining one hundred ways of quenching it, in none of which water took any part whatever. And as he allowed these delightful visions to play over him his eye roamed about carelessly over the tangle of cliff across the arc of the lagoon. A quarter of a mile away, one-third the way up the cliff, he seemed to see a speck of something which was neither cliff nor cactus. It might be the head and shoulder of a man who was kneeling up and peering round about over the top of a block of lava. Seaman Muller unslung his rifle and threw himself upon his face. He slipped a cartridge into the breech. The red splendour of the setting sun illuminated the speck of target presented to him. Muller was neither a good shot nor a musketry enthusiast. He took aim and fired just as he would have thrown a stone at a stray cat or bird. He did not even see whether he hit what he aimed at, for at the sound of the shot the empurpled face of a petty officer shot up from a hollow close beside him and an order bellowed into his ear roused even the undisciplined Muller to rise to his feet and sling his rifle and continue his slouching march back to the boats. And for firing the shot against orders he was very properly run into the punishment cells as soon as he and the Commander had reached *Ziethen* again.

But that last shot, fired in the last few minutes

of daylight, had reached its billet. The sharp-nosed bullet had hit Brown high up on the right shoulder; it had smashed a rib and a shoulder-blade on its way through, and had flung him back into his crevice. At first he was merely numb. He put his hands to his wound and was surprised to find them red with blood. It was some time before pain came—after the sun had set, in fact.

CHAPTER XIX

THE beginnings of Herr Schmidt's urgent calls had reached *Ziethen* soon after sunrise, but they were in a very mutilated form and so distorted that it could not even be guessed what cypher was being employed. The wireless telegraphist declared he could recognize the touch on the key of the main American agent, but this thin bit of evidence carried no weight. Only later was clear proof obtained that the message was in the Most Secret code, and from Schmidt himself, and it was nearly noon before the fragments of successive messages could be pieced together so that Captain von Lutz could read their dread import—that a British battle cruiser and light cruiser had passed the Panama Canal into the Pacific. As soon as he was sure of it there was no hesitation about his decisions. With certain death cruising after him in this fashion he was not going to linger within sight of land. He issued immediate orders for the recall of the landing party.

Nevertheless, as has been seen, those orders were more easily issued than obeyed. It was past three o'clock by the time that the inner landing party reached the ship with a fresh load of wounded and dead to madden those who had stayed on board, and by the time night fell on Resolution only the smallest driblets of the other force had trickled down to the boats; there were still nearly two hundred men hopelessly entangled on the slope. And with the coming of darkness the task of getting the weary men to imperil neck and limb by continuing the descent became hopeless. The petty officers blew their whistles and bellowed orders through megaphones into the night, but they did small enough good. Now and again a little group or a stray individual would come sliding down the last descent to where the boats lay, but the hours went by and the numbers on the cliff had not diminished very much. Messages flashed to *Ziethen* did nothing to allay the impatience of Captain von Lutz as he strode about fuming. With very little additional motive he would have taken the ship out and abandoned what was left of the landing party, but it was really too much to risk. Even if he had them all back, *Ziethen* would be perceptibly shorthanded, thanks to the casualties Brown had caused and the innumerable cut feet and sprained ankles incurred. The loss of another fifty men would be extremely serious, for Captain von Lutz had to bear in mind the prospect of strenuous coaling at sea and of sending away prize crews, to say nothing of having to fight further battles against hostile ships. He could not bring himself to abandon the stragglers, especially as it meant leaving them to certain death on a waterless island. He could only fret and fume and send orders to get the men into the boats as soon as possible, the while he calculated the chances of the British battle cruiser setting a course for the Galapagos and the time it would take her to get there.

The night wore through and morning came, and the broad light of day was pouring upon the tortured rocks before the last worn straggler came stumbling into the boats; it was almost high noon before *Ziethen* had her anchors up and was heading out of that accursed lagoon to the open sea with a depressed, weary crew and exasperated officers. For once the magnificent German efficiency had come to grief; the stern German discipline had failed. Much may be made of the rocks and thorns of Resolution, but some people are inclined to take most of the credit for the achievement away from these natural and incidental circumstances and bestow it upon Leading Seaman Brown, who had voluntary opposed himself to the might of an armoured cruiser, who had foreseen that the enterprise would cost him his life, and who had gladly paid this price without hope of applause for the sake of the Navy in which he served.

For Brown was dying surely enough. A night of torture had followed his wound. The pain came steadily, growing stronger and stronger as the crushing numbness following the initial shock had died away. He was in a high fever, and the dreadful pain made him heave and toss in pitiful, childlike efforts to get away from what was tormenting him. He had been thirsty enough before, but that thirst was nothing compared to the suffering he was now experiencing. Several times that night he had struggled back to consciousness, obsessed by an overwhelming thought that there might be a little water left in one of his two water-bottles. Each time he had writhed himself about until his left hand could grasp them and draw the corks and raise each in turn to his cracked and swollen lips. Once only—the first time—had this agonizing effort encountered success; three or four drops of fluid, cool and delightful, trickled out of the bottle's iron neck into his furred mouth, but that was all. There was never anything in either of the bottles afterwards, but Brown always hoped there was.

And as Brown held his left hand to his riven shoulder a troubled memory drifted into his mind of the German boy he had shot through the shoulder the day before yesterday. Brown's regretful mind recalled just how that boy had rolled out from behind his cover, trying to hold his shoulder together just as Brown was doing now. He remembered the frown of pain upon the boy's pleasant face, and he remembered how all day afterwards he had lain in the torturing sun with the flies thick about him, calling feebly in his unknown tongue for what Brown guessed must be water. Water ! Of course it was water for which he was asking. No one would dream of asking for anything else ; there was nothing else in all this world one-millionth part as valuable as water. The heartbroken cries of the German boy echoed in Brown's ears with pathetic persistence ; he heard them so long that he felt he must rouse himself to satisfy them. Once he had made up his mind to the effort it was easy enough. There had descended upon him a God-given ability to float quietly and without effort through the air ; it was so easy Brown was surprised he had not discovered it before. He floated down to where the German boy was lying, with the sun on his pale hair ; he took his hand, and the boy opened his eyes and smiled. It was such a friendly smile ; Albert loved him from that moment for the niceness of his blue, childlike eyes and his golden sunburn. Brown lifted him ever so easily just by the hand he held, and together they drifted away from the ugly sharp rocks into a place where there was pleasant shade The boy turned to him and made a gentle inquiry, and Brown nodded his head and said, "Presently." So they went on to where tall trees reared themselves up over a meadow of green grass, and there, beside the trees, there was a little, deep river of clear water; you could see it winding away over the green plain. And they drank of the water, and it was perfectly cool and wonderful. They drank and they drank, and they turned to each other and laughed with happiness, and then they lowered themselves into the clear depths and drifted with the stream, lapped about with water, in companionable nakedness. Everything was very friendly and happy and most blissfully perfect.

Then Brown turned and smiled to the pale-haired boy again, but he did not smile back. Instead his face was contorted with pain again, and he menaced Brown with his fists and glared at him with wild eyes, and Brown writhed back from him and found that the cool water had fallen away from around him, leaving him on the rocky bottom. And it was hot again, and the rocks beneath him were sharp—oh, and his shoulder hurt him so! With a start and a groan Brown came back to consciousness, to a dark world wherein flaming wheels hovered on his eyelids—a world of torment and agony and thirst, thirst, thirst.

The good things of this world had passed him by. He had never had an eye for the joy and wonder of a woodland triumphant with primroses or mysterious with bluebells. He had never known woman's love, not even bought love, and he had never known the love of a child, the touch of a tiny soft palm upon his cheek and fairy laughter. He knew nothing of the grim majesty of Lear nor of the sunny happiness of Twelfth Night. Good food and good wine and the glory of Rembrandt had alike passed him by. Never even had he known liberty; he had been all his life the slave either of a mother's ambition or of a Navy which demands her servitors' all to bestow upon unthinking ingrates. All his happiness, all his talents, his life itself, had been swept away in the tide of the Iron Age, the Age of the Twelve-Inch Gun. The achievements of Browr at twenty embraced nothing other than death and destruction. Brown might have died at eighty in a better-adjusted world and left behind him a long record of steady addition to the sum of human happiness, and the test of that might be whether he had not left behind any materials for a story. Yet if Brown had had the choice, just before his landing on Resolution, he would undoubtedly have selected for himself the career which has been outlined in these pages, and other people would have chosen the same for him too.

Brown never even knew the satisfaction of success; he never knew what stupendous results eventually crowned his efforts. Later on that last day he came back to consciousness; he swept the flies from his face and, under the impulse of his one consuming motive, he edged himself to the brink of the rock and peered out over the lagoon. The blue, blue water luxuriated in the drenching sunshine; the grim surround of cliffs danced and wavered in the shimmering heat before his reeling eyes. At the water's edge the marine iguanas browsed upon the seaweed as their Stone Age great-grandfathers had done. Far out at sea the gulls wheeled and sank over the grey line that marked the ocean currents' edge. But of *Ziethen* Brown could see nothing; the jagged cliffs cut off from his view the smudge of smoke which marked where she was heading out for the horizon. She had gone; she had got clear, and all Brown's efforts to detain her had only ended in a trivial forty-eight hours' delay, of no importance at all in a six months' cruise. Brown fell forward on to the rock again with a groan of broken-hearted despair, and flaming thirst and dreadful pain wrapped him about once more. They killed him between them, did pain and thirst, before the end of that day. He had been a plaguy long time dying, but he was dead at last.

CHAPTER XX

CAPTAIN RICHARD E. S. SAVILLE-SAMAREZ, C.B., M.V.O., sat alone in his cabin at his desk pondering the problems set before him by the terse Admiralty instructions received by wireless and cable, by the small Pacific chart before him bearing the estimated positions of von Spee and his squadron, and by the various possibilities which had gradually accumulated in his not highly imaginative brain. Of a surety his passage of the Panama Canal in H.M.S. *Leopard* with *Penzance* in company had caused very considerable stir. The Canal authorities had been dubious enough about letting him through, despite the fact that His Britannic Majesty's representative on the spot had made preparations for his arrival twenty-four hours before, quoting terms and treaties which declared the Canal open to all shipping whether in peace or war. Cables everywhere had been alive with the news when he entered the Canal; excited American papers would on the morrow be informing their readers that at last the British Navy had shown a sign of life instead of leaving hapless squadrons to be exterminated by von Spee. Already *Leopard's* presence would be notified to Berlin, and German diplomatists would protest the while the German Admiralty noted the information and weighed anxiously the effect of this slight dispersion upon the crushing superiority of the Grand Fleet at Scapa, where thirty Dreadnoughts awaited the emerging of the High Sea Fleet from its mine-fields and protected harbours.

Captain Saville-Samarez was not very different in appearance from what he had been twenty years before; he was not of the type that alters greatly with age. There were grey hairs now among his irrepressible brown ones, and authority and responsibility had brought character into his face; there were two firm vertical lines between his eyebrows, and his eyes seemed deeper set, and there was a grim line or two about his mouth, but he still seemed extraordinarily young, with his fresh complexion and upright carriage. Truth to tell, responsibility and authority sat lightly on his shoulders; he was never a man for deep thought or of much imagination, and the steadiness of his nerve had brought him out of whatever difficulties he had found himself in without any ageing flurry or worry. Little jobs like picking up moorings in a twenty-tousand-ton battleship in a crowded harbour with a full gale blowing he had simply accepted and carried through with automatically-acquired skill, and without any frightening pictures of what might happen if he made a mistake.

But just at present he was thinking deeply and trying his utmost to use all the imagination he possessed. He realized how fortunate he had been at present; the command of a battle cruiser was perhaps the biggest plum in the Service open to one of his rank. Moreover, he held an independent command at present, and the exigencies of the Service had put *Penzance* under his command as well. He grinned to himself at the recollection of the series of chances which had kept *Leopard* free from admirals—there were dozens of admirals who might have received the chance, and been glad of it, under some slight variation of circumstances. And an admiral would of course have gained the credit of any exploits *Leopard* might achieve, and Captain Saville-Samarez would be forgotten, forced to be content with a casual and inevitable reference in the official report.

Nevertheless, an admiral, while receiving the credit of success, would also have to bear the responsibility for failure, and in the absence of an admiral that responsibility would belong to Captain Saville-Samarez, and the Captain was almost worried about it. His instructions gave him a free enough hand; what he had to do was to hunt down von Spee and his squadron, concerting for that purpose with the other officers on the spot. The only tie upon him was the emphasis laid in his orders upon the necessity to keep *Leopard* from damage; no destruction of armoured cruisers would be worth the loss of a battle cruiser. To a staff officer such a condition would appear natural enough, as *Leopard* had an advantage of at least four knots in speed over any of von Spee's armoured cruisers, and her guns outranged any of von

Spee's by a couple of miles or more. But if *Leopard* by herself encountered von Spee with his three armoured cruisers all at once—*Scharnhorst*, *Gneisenau* and *Ziethen*—things might not be so easy. Two cruisers might close into range while he was sinking the third, or they might all scatter and he would be lucky to bag one of them, while the light cruisers would make themselves unpleasant simultaneously by trying to torpedo him. *Penzance* might get badly hit too, and that would be his fault as well. The rage of the British public if it heard that a damaged British ship had had ignominiously to seek internment in a neutral port would be unbounded.

So that a battle, were one to take place, would demand caution—it was this need for caution which was one of the factors worrying the Captain. And, all the same, a battle need not necessarily take place. Von Spee had last been heard of three thousand miles away, and to find a squadron hidden in three thousand miles of water was not an easy matter; on the contrary, it was an exceedingly difficult one. Von Spee might round the Horn and make a dash for home across the Atlantic and be halfway back before the news reached *Leopard;* he might even turn northward again and slip past *Leopard* and gain the Panama Canal—and that would mean Captain Saville-Samarez's professional ruin. The Captain realized that he needed all his wits to be sure of encountering the enemy.

And he wanted to encounter him too. With the age limit steadily pursuing him up the captain's list, he could see plainly enough that without something extraordinary happening he would just reach rear-admiral's rank before he had to retire. Unless he did something to distinguish himself he would end his life as rear-admiral on the retired list like fifty others he could name. He wanted to do something to make his name remembered, and the surest way would be to sink a German ship or two. Then the public would know him as "Saville-Samarez, the chap who caught von Spee," or "Saville-Samarez, you know, 'im 'oo sank the *Scharnhorst*"; and the Captain knew how valuable such a label tied on to him would be. It would be very handy if he went in for politics;

it might bring him a K.C.B.—and he wanted knighthood, for it had been the reward of his grandfather and great-grandfather before him. Above all, it might obtain for him a fat, comfortable colonial governorship on his retirement, and Saville-Samarez, with no means beyond his pay, urgently desired one. With the reward of success so rich, and the penalty of failure so severe, it behoved him to devote all possible energy to the solution of the problem.

Characteristically, however, he was making his final decision by himself. He had run through the meagre data with the Captain of *Penzance*, and heard his opinion, but he had left the final making up of his mind until he was alone. He did not shirk responsibility, and he had the utmost contempt for those who did—contempt which was only equalled by his contempt for councils of war in general.

He looked at the map, whereon von Spee was noted as last heard of at Valparaiso. He studied the scattered shipping lanes. He tried to get into von Spee's skin and work out what he would do in von Spee's position. He glanced once more through the last reports of the British secret agents. There was coal at German disposal in various South American Pacific ports, so that there was quite a sporting chance of von Spee returning northward. The wireless room of *Leopard* was continuously reporting hearing powerful messages in an unknown code, and it seemed extremely likely that they were warnings of his approach sent out to the German squadron. That made it possible that the German agents on the mainland thought it conceivable that German ships were near.

Now von Spee had fought at Coronel and had entered Valparaiso with only two armoured cruisers, *Scharnhorst* and *Gneisenau*. That was certain. Therefore his smallest armoured cruiser, *Ziethen*, had been detached before Coronel. Whither would von Spee be likely to send her? Northward? Not likely, with the whole Japanese navy on the look-out for her, and not much plunder to be obtained in the Northern Pacific. Westward, to the Indian Ocean? That was the richest field of all; but *Emden* was there already, and the English fleet could as well hunt down two cruisers as one. Besides, *Charybdis* lay on that route and had made no report of meeting German ships, although that was no real proof that *Ziethen* had not gone that way. (Captain Saville-Samarez did not appreciate the profound truth of this last deduction.) South-westward, to New Zealand and Australian waters ? Quite likely. But in that case Captain Saville-Samarez had no business with her ; his duty was to get into touch with the main body. But supposing *Ziethen* had not been sent anywhere like this ? Supposing she was still near the American coast ? Shipping certainly had not reported her, but she might have her own reasons for lying in concealment. She might have been in collision or had engine-room trouble. Certainly it was odd that she had neither fought at Coronel nor been reported elsewhere. Now supposing she had been damaged, where would she try and effect repairs ? Somewhere within wireless reach of Panama too, added Captain Saville-Samarez, making a false deduction from Herr Schmidt's activities without making allowance for that gentleman's supreme conscientiousness and ignorance of *Ziethen's* whereabouts. Captain Saville-Samarez looked at the map just as

Captain von Lutz had done a week before, and came to exactly the same conclusion. The Galapagos Archipelago presented the most opportunities to a ship in need of repair.

Captain Saville-Samarez went on to consider ways and means. The Archipelago lay a little out of his direct course south from Panama. But *Penzance's* most economical cruising speed was far in excess of *Leopard's*. The ships would overlook far more water separated than in company. And *Penzance's* speed was far larger than that of any one of von Spee's squadron, except perhaps *Dresden*. She could look after herself and keep out of danger by herself unless she experienced the very worst of luck—and Captain Saville-Samarez was not of the type which makes mental pictures of what might happen in the very worst of circumstances. He reached his final decision with promptitude, and did not think about it again. His signal flew for the *Penzance's* Captain to come on board *Leopard*, and a few quite brief sentences explained to that officer what Captain Saville-Samarez wanted done.

So that when the Captain of *Penzance* reached

his own ship again he set a fresh course which gradually took his ship away from *Leopard*, diverging slightly away to the westward as the two ships headed south across the Bay of Panama. Leading Seaman Albert Brown at this moment was only slightly thirsty; Muller's bullet did not hit him until sunset that day, when *Penzance* and *Leopard* had diverged until they were quite out of sight of each other.

CHAPTER XXI

NELSON once wrote that five minutes makes the difference between victory and defeat. It was hardly more than five minutes which made the difference between the detection of *Ziethen* and her possible escape from observation. Had *Ziethen* only sailed half an hour earlier she would have got away undetected to begin her career of destruction, and the history of the world—of the British Cabinet at any rate—would have been different. For as *Penzance*, detached by Captain Saville-Samarez to look round the Galapagos Archipelago, came down upon Resolution from the north-east, *Ziethen* was steering north-west away from the island. Just as Resolution came in sight a pair of keen eyes on *Penzance* detected a little trace of smoke far away on the westerly horizon. Smoke in that lost corner of the world was uncommon, and therefore suspicious, and *Pen-*

zance headed after it in all the pride of her twenty-seven knots. In half an hour *Ziethen* was definitely identified, and the ether was thrilling with the news as *Penzance* broadcast her information.

Vain it was now for *Ziethen* to try to jam *Penzance's* messages. *Leopard* was only a hundred miles away; besides, the men who built and equipped *Penzance* had a very clear idea of the duties she was to perform, which is more than can be said of those who built *Charybdis*. *Penzance* was one of the most modern of cruisers, designed solely to be of the utmost service to battleships. She was a battleship's eyes, a battleship's message bearer, and her immense speed and her powerful wireless installation were given her solely for these ends. Her news trickled in to *Leopard* hardly mutilated, and that great ship swung her twenty-thousand tons round in pursuit.

The Captain of *Penzance* knew his duty. Although his ship could match *Ziethen's* 6-inch guns with 6-inch guns of her own, it was not his business to put her fragile hull within reach when there was a battle cruiser no distance off who would do the business for him without any risk of damage. *Ziethen* was a bigger ship and carried armour far more effective than *Penzance's* fragile protective deck. *Penzance* could only possess the speed she boasted by reason of abandoning nearly all other protection; *Ziethen*, built in an age when the naval mind was a little muddled, had tried to combine all factors, speed (twenty knots at the time of her launching was a high speed), hitting power (German authorities did not place the same value upon large calibres as did the English) and armour, with the result that now she was helpless against a specialist.

She challenged action boldly enough; she wheeled, with her guns trained out upon *Penzance* and the range takers eagerly chanting the ranges; she charged forward, but *Penzance* was not inclined to accept the challenge. Not a man on board who would not gladly have fought *Ziethen* to the death, but what was the use of incurring senseless losses when *Leopard* was pounding up behind with her 12-inch guns, which would settle the matter without *Ziethen* having the chance of scoring a hit? *Penzance* kept away. Her seven knots advantage in speed was overwhelming No possible manœuvre of *Ziethen's* could inveigle her into range. It was not very long before *Ziethen* sullenly abandoned her attempt to make a fight of it and turned southwards at full speed in the hope of shaking off pursuit, or of closing in to a fight, when darkness came. And in reply to *Penzance's* reports *Leopard* turned away to a converging course, working up to her full twenty-four knots, edging rapidly up to the two ships which were cleaving their way through the blue Pacific.

It was then, perhaps, during the weary hours of that long pursuit, that Captain von Lutz tasted defeat and failure and self-contempt at their bitterest. One single man had caused this disaster; one man armed with a rifle had brought about the destruction of *Ziethen*. Captain von Lutz looked back over those three days at Resolution. A single one of them would have sufficed to repair *Ziethen* and set her off again upon her career of destruction. *Emden* had done ten million pounds' worth of destruction, and was still loose upon the

Indian Ocean. What of *Ziethen*, with her more powerful guns and armour? She had fought and sunk one miserable third-class cruiser thirty years old which mattered neither one way nor another in the clash of nations. Now, because one wretched English sailor had held her up at Resolution for forty-eight hours longer than was necessary, *Ziethen's* career was being ended. Captain von Lutz had no illusions about that. He knew that a battle cruiser and a light cruiser had passed the Canal; the light cruiser had arrived and was keeping him under observation, so that the battle cruiser could not be far away. And a battle cruiser would have no difficulty at all in setting the final seal on the work which Albert Brown had achieved at the cost of his life. The tea ships and meat ships and sugar ships, the ships carrying troops and the ships carrying bullion, would pass to and fro across the southern waters without *Ziethen* to sink them and burn them.

Yet although Captain von Lutz was so convinced of the approaching destruction of his ship, he had no thought of giving up the game without at least a final struggle. Vigorous messages passed to the engine-room, and soon *Ziethen's* boilers were filled up with every ounce of steam they could bear. Night was not far off, and if thick weather came with it *Ziethen* had a chance of escape, or, on the other hand, she might have a chance of closing with her adversaries and doing as much damage as she herself received. The pursuit must be prolonged until dark, and it was with an anxious eye that Captain von Lutz scanned the horizon as he paced about the bridge, the while officers and men laboured furiously making every preparation for a fight for life, stripping the ship of every conceivable combustible material, handling ammunition, and testing rangefinders and gunnery controls; such is the queer nature of mankind that the imminent prospect of a fight in which every single man of them might lose his life cheered them all up immensely, and the depression and indiscipline which had settled upon the ship after the ineffective attempts upon Resolution vanished like mist.

Night came while *Leopard* was still out of sight, and *Ziethen* began her attempts either to throw off *Penzance's* pursuit or else to close with her. But the night was clear, and *Penzance's* speed was one-third as much again as *Ziethen's*. An hour after nightfall the moon rose, and it was an easy enough matter for the look-outs on *Penzance* to pick up the loom of the big cruiser in the darkness. *Ziethen* turned sixteen points and came charging back straight up her own wake, but *Penzance* saw her and kept out of her way. *Ziethen* resumed her old course, maintained it for half an hour, and then turned two points to starboard. That time *Penzance* nearly lost her, but her great speed enabled her to zig-zag down the original course and find her quarry again. Before midnight the long expected help came—*Leopard* with her 12-inch guns and twenty-four knots. Then the two English ships were able to take up positions comfortably on *Ziethen's* port and starboard quarters so that the wretched cruiser's chances of escape, small enough to begin with, were now much less than half what they were.

All through the night the three ships drove on southwards through the Pacific. The Germans had no friends at sea within two thousand miles, and they were acutely and uncomfortably conscious of the menacing, silent presence of the British ships which were following after them, like Death on his pale horse. Twice already that night, in the hope that the shadowy cruiser which had hovered after them was within range, had they switched on searchlights and blasted the night with a salvo, but each time they had gained no profit from the performance save for the very definite comfort of noise and action. It seemed to temper down in their minds the terrible inevitability of the morrow.

But it could not be said that discipline was faltering. German naval *esprit de corps* was of new but sturdy growth. Every single man on board (for the rumour had run round, as lower-deck rumours will) knew that a battle cruiser was close upon them and that further resistance was hopeless, yet no word was breathed of surrender and hardly a man would have given his vote in favour of surrender. A young navy cannot afford to begin its traditions with a record of that sort. German sailors must fight to the death, so that those that follow after might have at least a glorious failure to look back upon. Four hundred men must die for that sole purpose; at least let it be recorded that they died not unwillingly.

With the first faint beginnings of daylight Captain Saville-Samarez gave orders to reduce speed below the nineteen knots at which *Leopard* had been ploughing through the sea since her junction with *Penzance*. He was going to take no chances, with those stringent passages from his instructions running in his mind. Daylight was not going to find him anywhere nearly in range of *Ziethen's* 6-inch guns. Even he, phlegmatic and confident though he was, had found the tension and excitement too great for sleep. He had been pacing about all night, the while the crackling wireless was sending through the relay ships to the Admiralty in Whitehall the glad news that one at least of the German Pacific Squadron was within the grip of the British Navy. Before dawn a reply had reached him, and he knew that the K.C.B. he desired would be his by the end of the year—if only he did what was expected of him.

And when daylight was almost come Captain von Lutz on *Ziethen's* bridge knew that his last hope was gone. Far away on the horizon, almost dead astern, his powerful glasses could make out through the clear atmosphere the unmistakable tripod mast of a Dreadnought battle cruiser. There was death in that insignificant little speck. Still there was some chance of doing damage. *Penzance* lay closer in, on the starboard quarter. *Ziethen* wheeled, with her guns reaching up to extreme elevation. As the sun's disc cleared the sea a crashing salvo broke forth from her side, but the range was too great. The columns of water where the shells fell rose from the surface of the sea nearly half a mile from the target. Five seconds later *Penzance*, in obedience to an irritated signal from *Leopard*, had turned away and was racing out of danger at her full twenty-seven knots, clearing the range for the 12-inch guns.

On *Leopard's* bridge stood Captain Saville-Samarez. The conning tower was no place for him during this affair. The whole business would be as dangerous as shooting a sitting rabbit; and Captain Saville-Samarez had taken *Leopard* into Heligoland Bight astern of *Lion*, and from the bridge had seen *Mainz* blown to pieces by the shattering salvoes. Now he saw

Ziethen swing eastwards, racing towards the level sun in one last hope of distracting the aim of the English gunners. But *Leopard* turned eastward too, steering a parallel course with the sun dead ahead and her guns training out to port. Eight 12-inch guns composed *Leopard's* main armament; and the 12-inch gun had twice the range of the 6-inch gun and fired a shell eight times as heavy, with a shattering effect twenty times as great.

Leopard turned two points to port to get *Ziethen* comfortably within range, resumed her original course, and battle began. One gun from each turret volleyed forth in its deafening, appalling thunder, and four 12-inch shells went soaring forth on their ten-mile flight. Each shell weighed half a ton, and between them they contained enough explosive to lay all the city of London in ruins. Woe betide *Ziethen* with her half-hearted attempt at armour plating and her fragile upper works!

"Short," said the Gunnery Commander up in the gunnery control tower, watching with detached professional interest the shooting of his beloved guns. "Up two hundred."

The other four guns bellowed in their turn, and the half-ton shells shrieked out on their flight—ten miles in half a minute, reaching two miles up into the air as they went.

"Short," said the Gunnery Commander again. The four immense columns of water were well this side of the racing armoured cruiser. "Up two hundred. This blasted climate's played Old Harry with the cordite!"

Punctually at twenty-five-second intervals the salvoes blared forth from the fifty-foot-long turret guns.

"Over," said the Gunnery Commander. "Short. Hit. Hit. Hit. Over."

Three times in a minute and a half *Ziethen* was struck by a ton of steel containing a ton of high explosive. The wretched ship's upper works were shattered and flung about, the steel plates were twisted and torn as though they were sheets of paper in a giant's hands. One shell burst fair and true on the breech of a starboard side 6-inch gun, wiped out the gun's crew and pitched the gun overside. But there was still life in the ship; the black cross still streamed out on its white ground from the tottering mast. Round she came, trying feebly to close with the enemy—just as, five days before, *Charybdis* had tried to do. But *Leopard* did as *Ziethen* had done then; she turned away at full speed, keeping her distance while the target slowly moved back abaft the beam. It was a hopeless effort to seek to close even to 6-inch gun range; there was no chance at all of being able to use torpedoes with effect.

"Hit," said the Gunnery Commander. "Over. Hit. Hit. My God!"

The 12-inch shells had blasted away great holes in the unarmoured upper works; one had blown a gap in the horizontal protective deck. The Gunnery Commander saw her lurching through the waves, smoke—furnace smoke, and shell fumes, and smoke from fires—pouring from every crevice; but she was still a ship; she still moved, she still floated; she might still fire her guns. But two shells from the last salvo crashed through the protective deck and burst amid her very vitals. Boilers and magazines alike exploded in one huge detonation. The rending flash was visible in the strong tropical sunshine for a tiny instant as the ship blew apart before the merciful black smoke bellied out and hid everything from view. Then, as this cleared before the fresh breeze, there was nothing to be seen, nothing. *Ziethen* had gone the way of *Good Hope* and *Monmouth*, the way *Scharnhorst* was to go, and *Defence* and *Black Prince*, armoured cruisers all, sunk with all hands by gunfire. Twelve salvoes had done it—hardly more than five minutes' firing. Every man on board had perished, including two Englishmen, the leading signalman and Ginger Harris, whom Brown had tended ; but of course the English ships did not know of their existence on board—and never would.

The black smoke eddied away, upward and to one side, and *Leopard* and *Penzance* raced for the spot where *Ziethen* had been. They found little enough : a dead man—half a man, rather—a few floating bits of wreckage, and nothing else. Iron ships stripped for action have little enough on board that will float. Then *Leopard's* triumphant wireless proclaimed the news far and wide—a welcome little victory, come just in time to counter the depression resulting from the defeat of Coronel, the sinking of *Cressy*, *Hogue* and *Aboukir*, and the depredations of *Emden*. It was England's proclamation of the mastery of the seas, to be confirmed within a week by *Sydney's* fortunate encounter with *Emden*, and within a month by Sturdee's annihilation of von Spee, where once again 12-inch guns blew armoured cruisers to destruction.

Then Captain Saville-Samarez was free to turn his ship back to England, to the misty North Sea for which he pined, and the prospects of "The Day." He was to take *Leopard* into the clamorous, bloody confusion of Jutland when the battle cruisers raced into action with *Lion* leading, and he was to stand watch and ward with the others amid the tempestuous Shetlands, but that was his great day. As he had foreseen, he became known as "the man who sank the *Ziethen*." But nobody was to know to whom the destruction of that ship was really due.

THE END